SADDLEBAG DISPATCHES MAGAZINE PRESENTS

UNDER ☙THE❧ COLD PRAIRIE MOON

OUTLAWS, IRON, AND VENGEANCE ON THE PLAINS

Saddlebag Dispatches, LCC
A Subsidiary of Oghma Communications
Bentonville, Arkansas
www.saddlebagdispatches.com

Under the Cold Prairie Moon: Outlaws, Iron, and Vengeance on the Plains
Description: First Edition | Bentonville: Saddlebag Dispatches, 2026
Identifiers: ISBN: 979-8-89299-133-9 (trade paperback)| ISBN: 979-8-89299-134-6 (eBook)
FICTION/Westerns | FICTION/Action & Adventure |
FICTION/Thrillers/Historical

Trade Paperback edition January, 2026

Cover Design and Interior Design by Casey W. Cowan
Editing by Anthony Wood, Dennis Doty, Don Money & Ben Henry Bailey

SADDLEBAG DISPATCHES MAGAZINE PRESENTS

UNDER THE COLD PRAIRIE MOON

OUTLAWS, IRON, AND VENGEANCE ON THE PLAINS

The Advance Guard by Frederic Remington

TABLE OF CONTENTS

Miner and Donkeys by W.H.D. Koerner

LIST ⚜ OF
ILLUSTRATIONS

Nearing the Fort by Charles Schreyvogel

PREFACE

———✦———

STOKE THE POT-bellied stove and pull up a chair, take a shot of rotgut and read tales of the Old West from some of the best writers in the genre. Welcome to *Under the Cold Prairie Moon*, coming to you from *Saddlebag Dispatches* Magazine, the award-winning magazine of all things western.

Learn that revenge is best served cold when a former lawyer tracks down the ruffians who murdered his family only to find out he killed the wrong outlaws. Take the trail with a piano player on a supply run who spoils an outlaw's attempt to steal the gold in a mining camp. Hide in the rocky hills near Deadwood with a wounded miner as an Indian closes in for the kill.

Stand tall with a young boy as he defends his family against a murdering thief. Follow a woman filled with raging revenge who survives a stagecoach robbery to seek out her lover's murderer. Help a sheriff investigate the grisly, fiery death of a molested woman and deliver her assailant to justice with the help of an experimental weapon. Hike into an old ghost town with an uncle and four kids only to find yourself transported to the Old West where villains abound on every turn. Help a lady journalist wrestles with the decision whether to expose lynching justice or not in a small town for all to read. Traipse behind a 90 year old retired postal worker and his favorite bronc until he comes to terms with his own death.

Do you want to know what the Old West truly was like? Ponder these tales and yarns straight out of the hills and prairies from great writers lie Paul Lewis, Michael Mitchell, Rick Sapp, Michael F. Mc-Donnell, Maureen Rose Callahan, Leigh Alver, John Tures, Jeanine M. Frois, and Jason Rodriguez. I guarantee you will be the better for it.

—Anthony Wood
Managing Editor, *Saddlebag Dispatches*
November 15, 2025

SADDLEBAG DISPATCHES MAGAZINE PRESENTS

UNDER THE COLD PRAIRIE MOON

OUTLAWS, IRON, AND VENGEANCE ON THE PLAINS

A Sioux Chieftan by Frank Tenney Johnson

BUFFALO SOLDIER

ABIGAIL DOTZLER

THE BUFFALO ARE almost gone now. Hunters have shot, killed, and skinned them to near extinction. No one cares. The buffalo's dwindling numbers only make their hides and tongues more valuable. One hide puts twice as much food on my table as it did ten years ago. Supply and demand, the traders call it. I don't know much about business, but hunting God's creatures until there ain't any left seems wrong. Starving seems worse, though.

With my back to the rising sun, I thumb my hat up and lope across the prairie. Less buffalo and more hunters make my job that much harder too. Higher chance some hapless kid spooks and shoots me. Higher chance some Southern boy still bitter about the War takes his vengeance on me. Ain't my fault the Rebs lost. I was born north of the Mason-Dixon, and I've been free my whole life. Doesn't matter much out here in Kansas though.

A herd of cowboys sweep by, scaring off my buffalo. They sold their cattle, and now they aim for a sabbatical in Dodge City. Gambling, whores, alcohol, and any other vice you can name—Dodge has it. All the money those cowboys just earned will be gone come sundown. I stay clear of Dodge. Ain't got money to waste, and plenty of bitter hunters are willing to kill for a buffalo's tongue. Though I don't much care for the taste myself, I reckon the traders ship the tongues out east where the high-falutin folks who eat them can pretend they didn't come from a living, breathing creature.

Trotting onward, my horse and I crest a hill. Three buffalo roll in the wallow, deepening the depression. Some water has gathered, and a buffalo with a hide of purest white bends to drink. A hide like that, once cleaned of the dirt that streaks through the cloudy fur, would set me and my family up for life. My children will never go without dinner again. How much more will the traders pay for an albino buffalo tongue? A valuable hide like that will put a target I don't need on my back.

A wooden stake marks an otherwise unnoticeable grave not far from the temporary watering hole. The prairie grass grows a little taller on the low-rising mound. The poor son of a gun likely got himself shot by a drunken cowboy, bit by a snake, or trampled by a stampede. The frontier's border pushes ever westward, but life still ain't easy in Kansas. The white buffalo ambles closer to the grave to munch on the grass.

I brace my rolling block rifle against my shoulder and take aim at one of the wallowing bison. The white hide will likely only get me killed. Hunters can be the jealous sort, and many a man in Dodge don't take kindly to being shown up by anyone, much less someone like me. The single shot plows through the buffalo's thick skin, burrows into its heart, and snuffs out the creature's life. It's a quick death. My aim is true. The others, two plain and unnoteworthy, one white and priceless, startle and race for the next wallow. In their haste, they leave plenty of tracks, and I take my time thumbing another round into the rolling block.

It's an old gun, issued to me by the U.S. Cavalry during the War. I didn't want to serve, but my brothers pressed me into it. None of them lived to regret it, though, as I am the last of Mama's boys still standing. We hardly saw any battle. My brothers were killed by jealous, bitter men, fellow Yankees, our supposed brothers in arms. I survived the lynchings. I survived Saltville. Much of the Fifth Colored Regiment was slaughtered then. I thought I saw enough of death then, but there's always more blood on the horizon.

My horse and I trot down the hill to the bison's corpse. It's still gasping for air. My aim wasn't as true as I thought. Unsheathing my Bowie, I plunge the knife into the creature's neck and let the blood run over my hands. Its last breaths are slow, but shallow. I bow my head and place my bloodstained hand on its wide nose, thanking the buffalo for its sacrifice. Only through its death can my family live. Vultures already gather in the sky above, and there's nothing left to do but get to skinning.

After the Fifth was disbanded and my brothers buried, Mama couldn't bear to see me, the last of her boys. I was too painful a reminder of what she had lost. So, I joined the new Tenth Colored Regiment and patrolled the Great Plains. They called us Buffalo Soldiers, and I saw plenty of death there too

With the hide free, I roll it and secure it to the back of my saddle. My horse is large and strong, another souvenir from the War. An officer in the Fifth, a white man like all officers, had owned the horse. When a Rebel bullet gave him gangrene, I took the horse. He can carry my weight and several buffalo hides with no issue. The honest traders try to buy him from me. The hunters, never to be shown up, try to steal him. I find the tracks of the bull group that ran off. One set sinks deeper into the soft dirt from a heavier creature. The white one if I were a betting man. Bidding the dead man in his shallow grave goodbye, I mount my horse, and we set off at a steady pace. My horse serves well and doesn't mind the stench of blood or the noise from my rolling block. He knows the business of killing. It don't make a difference to him if we're killing men or bison. I don't know if it makes a difference at all.

My sister says I'm cursed. She says the night I was born was a bad one—rolling thunder with no rain, green skies with no other signs of a twister. The critters were silent, except for a cow who birthed a two-headed calf. The calf didn't make it till morning, and my sister tells me Mama didn't think I would either. My brother's wife named me Sue as a joke. When I stubbornly held onto life, Mama, being tired of boys, kept the name. I tell my sister that a name like that is enough of a curse, but she says that it's more than an awful name. Never made much sense to me, but now I wonder as I wipe the bison's blood on a clump of buffalo grass if she doesn't talk more sense than we give her credit for.

The white hide will give the other hunters more than enough reason to see me to my Maker. Some cur might see the pale fur stacked against the browns and blacks tied to my saddle and might decide his paycheck is worth more than my life, just as I decided mine is worth more than the bison's. But if I can manage to kill the beast and survive any attacks, the money will provide for my family for months. Combined with the three other hides and tongues, I may even have enough to waste. After all these long nights on the prairie, after all my years serving this country, one drink in Dodge is well-earned.

Fool talk, that's all. It never stopped at one drink, just as it never stopped at one life.

Shod hoofprints from this morning's cowboys bury the buffalo tracks. I jump out of the saddle, adding my own prints to the mix, to pick the bison's out. The deep ones, from the albino, stand out the best. The other two likely followed it. With any luck, the white buffalo will lead me to a whole herd, not that there's many of those left. The sun rises higher as I track the buffalo. My hat does what it can to prevent the light from burning my eyes, but it ain't much. I raise my hand to block the sun. The tracks are getting harder to follow, and the heat ain't helping my focus. The hide's stench is worse.

I cross paths with a few hunters. None look happy to see me, as most haven't got a single shot off yet. Years ago, a hunter could count on fifty hides or more by sundown. Five seems a better estimate these days. With my horse showing theirs up, the hunters glare at me. They check the smaller Colts hanging from their hips when I stoop to examine the white buffalo's tracks. Some try to make conversation, waving or shouting "howdy" or asking after my wife. I don't know their names, and I don't know how they know mine. I stopped learning names after Saltville. The plains are overrun with hunters. I reckon there are more of us than buffalo. I imagine their surprise when I come back this way with the white hide. They won't be able to show me up. Any of these men would kill me just as soon as offer me a drink of water. A man has to do what a man has to do. Risk and reward, I think I heard it called.

I've always been told that killing's wrong, and I can't help but agree. It's always been something I got to do. Men or bison, in battle or on the plains. I don't much care for the business, but I track the three buffalo away from the herd of hunters. They roamed far. The albino in the lead, he's a smart one. Smarter than most hunters give the creatures credit for. Reckon that's how he's managed to avoid his fate. I hate to be the one to bring fate to him, but my horse and I slow to a stop a couple hundred yards from another wallow.

The albino buffalo rolls in the dust, caking his white hide in brown. A good scrubbing and the hide'll be right as rain. When my son was a boy and my wife pulled him from the bath, he would dart for the nearest patch of dirt and roll around, coating himself. Said he wanted to be a Buffalo Soldier, like me, only he didn't know what that meant. He'd seen buffalo in their wallows, however, and made his best guess. He joined the Ninth Cavalry and lost his arm fighting Indians. I edge my horse closer to the wallow, and the white bison ends his dust bath. He lumbers to his feet, sensing me.

Instead of running, however, he just stares. The two unnoticeable bison amble to their leader. I check my rolling block and aim for the one furthest to my left. The shot will scare the remaining plain bison, but the albino will be easiest to track. I am prepared to track him across the continent. My horse and I are cut from the same hardy cloth. The albino snorts, and my aim drifts to him. His head is raised. He ain't scared of me.

I knew an officer back in the War who was slaughtered with his men. He retreated once but refused to be backed into a corner by the Rebs. He ordered the soldiers to fight. He was the first man in battle himself. He was outnumbered, but he wasn't scared. He looked death in the eye, and I watched a bayonet spear his heart. I'm sure the good men he got killed would rather he'd chosen retreat.

My horse paws at the ground. He knows I have a good shot and can't figure why I don't just take it. The two bison wander away from the albino, who is still. He looks like one of them marble statues the fancy folk out east got, but his eyes focus on mine. He looks like that officer. He looks like all the Rebs and Indians I killed with the cavalry.

I ain't seen an albino buffalo before today. He might be the only of his kind. It seems a shame to take his life, but the food he'll put on my table, the drinks he'll buy me in Dodge, and the looks on the traders' faces as I drag in a pure white hide will have to make it worth it.

I aim for his heart. The blood'll wash out. He ain't the first sorry soul I've killed, and I know he won't be the last, what with this curse hanging over my head. It's the curse that pours blood on my hands.

I couldn't tell a soul why this murder felt any different. A tear carves a line through the dust caking my face as I squeeze the rolling block's trigger.

—Before she could write, Abigail Dotzler would hand her mother a pen and paper and dictate stories, insisting that her mother transcribe her words exactly. Though she grew up addicted to fantasy novels, the American West called to her, and after seeing Tombstone, she fell in love with westerns and promptly filled her bookshelves with Wyatt Earp biographies and Louis L'Amour novels. She studies Creative and Professional Writing at the University of Wisconsin-Whitewater, where she serves as the co-editor-in-chief of The Muse, the university's literature and arts magazine. When she isn't scribbling her stories or reading the classics, she loves to take long walks in the woods and wander through museums.

BURNT

LEE CLINTON

LAS CRUCES, NEW MEXICO TERRITORY
1893

BY THE TIME I got to see the body, it had been pulled clear of the ashes. The torso lay on its side with a lassoed rope under the arms, which now reached out as if to embrace. The sight was disturbing, not just from the grotesque shape of rigid twisted limbs, but the gruesome smile of white teeth in a blackened skull. Added to this was the pungent smell of burnt flesh and hair that lingered in the air and caught in the throat, a putrid odor that clung to clothing. It was as if death was trying to attach itself to the living.

I didn't know her. The charred corpse was just a name, Sara Prescott, but to her neighbors she had been living flesh and blood. A young woman in her prime. Now they whispered of the tragedy, a terrible act of fate. Me? I didn't know how or why this had happened, but I knew it had nothing to do with fate.

When all had left, I remained and watched the buckboard creak down the track through the mud. The wheels slipped into the furrows with a jerk as the body, now covered by canvas, rocked from side to side. The deputy wanted to stay, but I told him that he needed to deliver the remains to the undertaker and assist the town doctor. He looked lost and I knew why. He was having trouble holding it together, and had I been in his shoes at that age, with his experience, or lack of it, I would have felt the same too. But this was not my town, and these were not my people—not yet.

I had arrived just three days prior as a replacement, sent down from Santa Fe by order of Bill Thornton, the newly appointed Territory Governor. I didn't know it at the time, but Thornton was worried that the Santa Fe Ring had established a presence in Las Cruces. I was just told that Sheriff Roy Kendall, who was in hospital in San Bernardino, wasn't returning to duty and that his deputy needed help. Being at loose ends, I got the job.

It was a relief.

I knew I was being eased out and didn't want to go. What the hell was I going to do with my time, or what was left of it, sitting on the porch watching the world go by. So I saddled up with a smile and followed the Rio Grande down to the southern border, all the time knowing that this would be my last hoorah.

I poked around the ruins, starting in the cookhouse as most fires come from a ready-made source. The cast iron stove stood alone on its pedestal, the top, still warm, and the firebox door open. Directly below was a pile of ashes close to where the fire poker lay upon the ground. It was twenty-three steps away from where the body of Sara Prescott had been found, on her cot in the front chamber, the remains of her small dog close by. The toe of my boot kicked against a small glass bottle, which I picked up. I had known this little bottle well, and slipped it into my coat pocket.

The funeral took place three days later. I stood at the back, collar up against a biting wind. It was hard to hear the preacher, and I couldn't figure out who was family, as no one stepped forward to openly show grief. It was as if attendance came from habit.

The town doctor was there. We had yet to meet, but I knew of his reputation. He served with John Bell Hood as a surgeon during the war.

Gossip in the days before the funeral said that he had to use his skills to saw off the stiff protruding limbs to fit the body into the coffin. It may have been so. I'd known worse.

Introducing myself at the conclusion of the graveside service, I asked, "Can you tell me anything that I need to know about the deceased?"

His reply was abrupt, "Like what?"

I handed him the bottle.

His manner was moderate. "Oh, that. I prescribe those for toothaches."

"She had a toothache?" I sarcastically asked.

He paused before replying. "No, but she was in pain."

"She must have been, this once contained thirty opium tablets. I was put on these after being wounded at Yellow Tavern. Took me years to leave them alone."

"Yellow Tavern, ah, who was your commander?"

"Jeb Stuart."

"Cavalry?"

I nodded.

"Where were you wounded?"

"Upper leg."

"Figures. Removed a lot of legs from wounded cavalry men." He paused before asking, "You now looking into this death then?"

I nodded again.

He held up the bottle. "And you found this?"

"Next to her cot."

"Can I trust you?"

"To do what?"

"Keep looking."

It was an odd request, but I confirmed that I would.

"She had been hurt, hurt bad, internals, suspected broken ribs. I could see she'd been beaten, but she wouldn't let me examine her. I also suspect that she'd been...."

I waited.

Finally, he said, "molested."

"Do you know who did it?"

"Not that I can prove."

"But you can guess?"

"Serious allegation to accuse a man of that. Best you find the evidence yourself."

MY LODGINGS WERE a small cabin just out the back of the sheriff's office. Pleasant, clean, and surrounded by the personal possessions of Sheriff Kendall. My deputy, who was newly married, lived nearby and extended an invitation to Sunday dinner. I jumped at the chance of a home-cooked meal and the opportunity to hear about the community. The evening was most pleasant, and the boiled chicken and cranberry gravy were excellent. But every time I mentioned the name Sara Prescott the conversation went quiet.

The following Sunday I attended church, not that I am a man of religion, although I have been known to pray when my luck ran thin. All the pews were full, so I had to squeeze in down the back, making it uncomfortable for all in that row. The sermon was the normal gloom and doom as the congregation passively nodded in agreement. At the conclusion of the service, I did my best to mix but had little luck. It was clear that I was the uninvited guest. When walking back toward my cabin, I spied a woman with two young children in tow and took the opportunity to introduce myself. Her name was Beth Hall and around her shoulders was a black widow's shawl.

"Can I walk you anywhere? Home?"

"Sheriff, you would have a long walk back, I live four miles out of town."

I was confused. "So how are you getting there?"

"Walking."

"With the little ones?"

"They are strong."

"You have no carriage?"

"No."

I looked back up at the congregation, "And no one has offered...."
She shook her head.

"Then let me. I have a buckboard at my disposal."

Her words were guarded, and I had to resort to direct questions on our journey. "Did your husband pass recently?"

"He disappeared," was the curt response.

"So, he's not passed?" I asked.

"His body has never been found, but I can tell you that David would never have left his family of his own accord."

"Do you want to tell me what you know?"

"I know little, can prove less, but suspect a lot."

"You want to tell me?" I asked.

"Do you want to hear?'

"I do."

"My husband fell afoul of Desmond Quinn. He was the holder of our mortgage and foreclosed. We lost everything, including the father of my children."

The name Desmond Quinn was new to me. "Quinn?" I asked. "You are the first to mention that name."

She gave a wry smile. "How often do you go to church but never hear mention of the devil? Yet he's the one doing most of the sinning."

It was a point I couldn't dispute.

She went on to say, "James four, verse seven says, resist the devil and he will flee, but no one will resist Quinn. They are frightened, and who could blame them? They just have to look at me."

I STARTED TO ask about Desmond Quinn, but all seemed uneasy, with some breaking off the conversation without so much as a by-your-leave. Others just avoided me on sight, often walking across the street. When I was summoned late at night to the back room of the Luna Vista Cantina, I knew what was at hand, but it was no less unsettling. The lamps were dimmed and the place crowded with *vaqueros*. All were rough, cocky, and eyeing me over. I quickly did a headcount. There were twelve, and Quinn made thirteen.

Sitting at a round table, cards in hand and smoking a cheroot, Desmond Quinn pointed to where I should stand. "I hear you've been asking about me, so what have you got on your mind, Sheriff?"

This was a setup to intimidate. I'd been here before, and it only happens when you are being warned off. Inadvertently, Quinn had just incriminated himself. Whatever he was guilty of, he didn't want me to find out.

"I wanted to know where you fit into this town," I said in a measured voice.

"I fit in just fine. The trouble is, you don't. Especially when you go making people uneasy by asking a whole lot of questions. All you need to do, Sheriff, is mind your own business, and we'll get along fine. If not, then you're likely to get burnt."

This amused the cowboys who all grinned.

"Sounds simple enough," I said.

Quinn smiled.

I pushed my hat back a little to better see. "But that's not how it works. I've been sent here by the governor to uphold the law, and that's what I intend to do." I touched the brim to bid farewell, turned, and withdrew.

On returning to my cabin, I had to grip my fists to stop my hands from trembling. I was getting too old for this. I'd been served notice but had managed to state my position. However, it was all bluff. If they wanted to run me out of town, they could, anytime they chose. Or Quinn could just make me disappear like Beth Hall's husband. She had referred to Quinn as the devil. I didn't know if he was, but if his intent was to menace with evil, it had worked.

The following night, a shot was fired into my cabin. It was a message. A warning that life was getting dangerous in Las Cruces.

THE NAME HEINRICH Volz was written in faded yellow letters on his high sided wagon. Below that was Travelling Gunsmith.

I took the opportunity to have him examine all the firearms in stock and gauge them for serviceability.

"Most are in good order, some need repair, but all are getting old. Maybe you need some new weapons."

I wasn't really listening. Quinn was overshadowing my every thought. I had wanted to send off a telegram to Santa Fe seeking information and advice, but could I trust the telegraph office not to inform Quinn? I thought not.

The gunsmith repeated his words.

This time he got my attention. "Repairs, yes, fine."

He came closer and in a soft voice with a Prussian accent said, "Have you ever seen one of these?"

I looked. "No."

"It's a metal jacketed bullet."

He dropped it into my hand. The case was large and narrowed like a bottleneck to a long silver bullet. It was weighty but sleek with a centre-fired primer at the base.

"Uses a smokeless powder so it does not give away the position of the firer, and it's fast, 2,000 feet per second."

I couldn't take my eyes off its sleek gleaming presence. "What's the caliber?"

"The bullet diameter is measured in millimetres, 8.19 or .32 inch as you know it."

"Looks nasty. Is it a hunting round?"

"Hunting men. It's military ammunition and with this metal jacket it will pass right through a body, and if someone happens to be standing behind the man who has just been shot, then it will continue on and wound him severely."

"And the rifle?" I asked.

"The latest in Austrian arms. I have a friend." He reached back. "Called a Mannlicher after its designer. This is the carbine, for the cavalry, shorter than the rifle, under forty inches in length. See this?"

He pointed to the underside of the rifle, forward of the trigger guard. "It's the magazine."

I looked carefully. "How do you load it?"

"Let me show you." He pulled straight back on the bolt, picked up a brace of five rounds stacked one upon the other in a metal clip and dropped it into the open breach, and with his thumb, pushed down.

I watched the bullets and clip disappear into the magazine. "Do that again," I said.

He ejected the rounds and the clip by pressing a small release in the trigger guard and repeated the demonstration.

"Ingenious," I said.

"It is," he said. "But the best is yet to come. This is a beautiful weapon to fire, finely balanced and accurate. Do you want to try?"

"Yes," I said, "I certainly would."

I rode with him just out of town and into the wide-open spaces. We alighted, and he handed me the carbine. It was indeed well balanced, comfortable to the shoulder, and on firing gave a firm kick as it propelled the large bullet down range. I reloaded with a simple pull and push of the bolt. On ejecting the fourth spent case, the clip also ejected, allowing for a quick and simple reload after the fifth shot. This was indeed an exceptional weapon, and accurate, as I consistently hit targets out to 300 yards.

"That's nice shooting. Are you impressed?" he asked.

"Yes," I said. "A weapon like this could make all the difference in a battle."

I FOUND THE folded letter under my door. It had been placed there sometime on Sunday and simply addressed, Sheriff—along with the message—Best you leave while you can. No one will help you. They never helped me or poor Sara. All are frightened. Besides, you can't change anything. It was signed, Beth.

I visited the town doctor the following day and presented the message. "Is this evidence?" I asked.

He looked a little bewildered. "What's this?"

"You wanted evidence? Read it."

He did, carefully. "Maybe it's just good advice."

"Beth Hall's husband disappeared. People don't just disappear. She's shunned by her neighbors and now she mentions Sara Prescott."

The doctor was uneasy.

"The firebox door of the stove was open. The coals had been raked out. Sara was out of it on opium tablets and unable to save herself if she wanted to."

"Then you know as much as I do. But what are you going to do about it?"

I RODE OUT to Beth's with her letter tucked inside my coat. She was hanging out the laundry when I arrived. "I got your letter," I said, "you want to tell me more?"

"What's more to say? You've been asking too many questions. Quinn doesn't like that. You will disappear, just like my David."

"Did Quinn kill Sara Prescott?"

"Quinn doesn't kill anybody. He just makes problems go away and has others do the killing."

"Why Sara?"

"I would be willing to tell you if I thought it might do some good. If it was to get Sara justice, but it won't. There is nothing you can do."

"Try me. Was Quinn involved?"

She nodded as I stared back at her in silence before turning to go. I had my foot in the stirrup when she called, "Quinn was using Sara for his pleasure. She told me so. She also told me she was with child."

The ride back was one of wild thoughts. The evidence was not enough for an arrest, let alone a conviction. It was hearsay, but my gut told me it was true. About a mile on, I stopped at the top of an eroded wash flanked by mesquite. I surveyed the dips and folds before easing out of the saddle to walk the ground, marking three locations to form a triangle, each with a clear view while offering protection from both observation and fire. It was what a soldier would call defendable killing ground. Only then did I catch my callous considerations. What was I doing? There had to be a better way than this I told myself.

Trouble was, I couldn't think how.

"I SAW YOU alter your aiming point off a little to the right the other day to hit each target fair center. Let me adjust the sights for you." The gunsmith used the blade of a small screwdriver. "Unfortunately, I don't have a lot of ammunition. How much do you need?"

"Thirteen rounds, if I shoot straight."

"Thirteen targets and just you?"

"Just me."

"And what will these targets be trying to do?"

"Kill me."

"I only have fifteen rounds. You will have to shoot very straight. Can you do that?"

"I have no choice."

"To save yourself?"

"To save this town."

"One against thirteen sounds like a war."

"I'm a sheriff, not a soldier."

"You may be a sheriff, but if you are at war, you need to act like a soldier."

THE TELEGRAM WAS brief and to the point. It was addressed to the Governor's office and requested any known information on Desmond Quinn in relation to the disappearance of David Hall. I knew it wouldn't be sent, but that was not its purpose. I just wanted a reaction, and it didn't take long.

Quinn's men started assembling outside the Luna Vista, and one of them peeled off to follow me as I rode out toward Beth's place. He followed me for about a mile then returned to town. I continued on to the ground I'd surveyed. With me were three full canteens. I placed two of these at the flanks positions I had previously selected and kept one over my shoulder. Also over my shoulder was a leather bandolier containing my precious fifteen rounds of ammunition in three clips of five.

The Mannlicher carbine remained in its scabbard on my mount, now tethered off to the rear behind cover and out of sight, while I moved to the highest point from where I could look back toward town. I now waited, and in less than an hour the dust could be seen rising about half a mile out. I took a long drink, went back to my horse, looped the canteen over the saddle, and pulled the carbine free. On weaving my way to the center forward position of my triangle, I loaded the first clip and counted the thirteen bobbing heads as they rode into view, bunched until the trail entered the wash, forcing them into a neat single file. I couldn't see Quinn, so I guessed he was somewhere in the middle. Taking up a crouching firing position, I sighted on the leading man, checked my breathing, and squeezed the trigger.

The first man fell from his horse to the sound of the shot as it echoed down the gully. My next four rapid-fire shots each hit their mark dead center as the clip ejected from the magazine. I dropped down flat into a shallow crevice just as the returning fire ricocheted off to my right. I went left, crawling like a lizard, the carbine in the crook of my arms. The fire continued as I reached my flank position and rolled onto my back, pulling a clip from the bandolier. The firing continued as I reloaded, but none of it was in my immediate vicinity. I gulped a drink from the fresh canteen, then crouched, easing up to take a look. One of the *vaqueros* was brave enough to make a move, but he was too quick for me to take a shot. I knew where he had gone to ground and sighted up. He lifted his head looking forward, and I squeezed off my sixth shot. He vanished as a volley of return fire was let loose, but it was wild and inaccurate. Just wait, I told myself, just wait. Two figures at the rear sought to make their escape, backs turned as I accurately squeezed off the next two rounds. Across to the far flank another two made their move forward, crouching. I dropped the first one but missed the second. "Damn," I heard myself say as I reloaded my last clip.

Shouting started about thirty yards away. It was Quinn trying to muster his troops. Two stood as one to better see and I fired. One fell as the other went to ground. It was then that a single rifle shot came into my position and pierced the water canteen. I immediately knew why, the sun had reflected off the metal neck, giving away my position. I took off fast and low, drawing fire as I tried to make my way to the far flank, only to be pinned down halfway. My plan to use the third firing position had gone astray.

By my reckoning, I had killed or wounded ten and had just three rounds left in the magazine. I could not afford a shootout, so I drew my handgun and fired two shots to distract. As the blue gun smoke caught the wind, it exposed my position and the incoming fire intensified.

Stupid! What was I thinking?

I squirmed on my back toward the right, then drew up slowly on one knee. The firing continued, now very close, as I heard the scrambling of footsteps. Three figures appeared immediately before me, two forward and one back. I fired instinctively, first left then right, the butt pressed to the side of my body as the clip ejected from the magazine. I had just one round left.

I waited, dry mouthed, before gradually easing myself up to see three fallen bodies, but exactly who had been hit by my fire? A soft murmur could be heard. I knew that sound, it was one of the wounded. The two closest to me lay dead but behind them was Quinn, slumped and clutching both hands to his bleeding stomach. A bullet had passed through the body of one of the dead to find its mark. I looked down at the pallid face and quivering lips.

"Help me," came the pathetic plea, "I'm hurt bad."

"I can see," I said as I turned to go.

He called after me with effort, "Have you no mercy."

I didn't answer. What he now begged for, had been denied to David Hall and Sara Prescott. Yet, at that moment, we were both without moral virtue. I had also shown no mercy to those who had been lured into my trap. On judgement day, neither of us would be able to justify our sins, but at that moment it mattered little to me. I had extinguished the flames of hell that burnt the innocent, and that had been my intention.

I weaved my way back across the broken ground, returning to each firing position to retrieve the canteens and every spent cartridge case and clip. When finished, I was on the high side of the ravine where I could look back down on the killing ground. Silently, I counted each of the twelve dead where they lay. Quinn waved as if to let me know that he was still there. I waved back before lifting the carbine to my shoulder for one final shot.

—The author is an Australian writer of ten Western novels published under the pen name of Lee Clinton as part of the Black Horse Western (BHW) series. While this line of books has now been discontinued by the publisher, such titles as Reins of Satan, The Proclaimers, and Reaper are still available in digital form via Amazon. In the meantime, the writing of short stories allows the author to continue his love of the American Western.

Saving the Mail by Charles Schreyvogel

TREE OF JOSHUA

JEANNE M. FROIS

BASED ON A TRUE STORY

HUGH MCPYLE WAS dead.

Dead and nobody had cut him down yet. He swung like a pendulum on a clock, the rope around his neck creaked in the wind, and sounded like lost seconds ticking away into eternity. The twisted hanging tree stood on a windswept hill behind which rose another barren hill with a church that wore a white steeple as its crown.

The late November day was colored in charcoal, dun, and pewter. The wind that barreled down from the mountain through the nearby leafless woods teased the church bell into periodic, almost hesitant clangs.

Hugh's stiff body twirled in a windy dance in three quarter time. An onyx flock of crows had landed in the nearby field and stood biding their time.

Rose emerged from the woods astride old Whittaker, a pretty, slender, young woman atop the old horse. Whittaker, gray like the day, was spotted in black and white as if someone had gotten careless with paint buckets and Whittaker got in the way.

Rose, seeing Hugh McPyle hanging from the tree before a church,

jerked to a stop. When she needed to think, Rose took long contempla-
tive rides with no definite destination in mind. Today, like a nightmare
that suddenly looms in the middle of blissful sleep, she and Whittaker
had wandered off the beaten path straight to a dead man dangling from
a tree in front of a church.

Outraged, several oaths that would have made her seaman grandfather blush remained unuttered. Sometimes, Rose had thoughts like
a man, but at heart she was always a lady—with a steely spine.

———————◆◆◆◆◆———————

SARAH ROSE O'MALLIE was nineteen years old and lived in the
neighboring town of Vainglory, Texas, with her father Logan who ran
the local newspaper. Since the death of his wife nearly two years before,
Logan sprawled in his office chair in a perpetual drunken stupor, yet the
townspeople were amazed at the quality of writing that the Vainglory
Herald produced without fail each day. In fact, since the death of his
wife, the stories had expanded to improve an editorial viewpoint that
savaged the treatment of Indians and all things unjust. The Eastern papers had tipped their hats to the editorials by reprinting many of them.
No one connected any of the change to the arrival of Rose returning
home from school to take care of her father, a revelation that would
put them out of business for certain.

She rode up to the minister's house next to the church and glanced
down the main street of the small town finding it suspiciously deserted
for early afternoon.

Her knock was answered by a small, dark-haired woman whose
pale blue eyes bore into the amber eyes of Rose and disapprovingly
took in her long red skirt, black broadcloth blouse, fawn colored man's
duster, and sun-streaked brown braid trailing on her shoulder. The
woman stared at the full scarlet skirt in pointed disapproval. Rose
smiled, realizing she had been labeled a hussy on the spot. The woman
sniffed in disdain.

"What do you want?" asked the woman.

"I want to see the minister," Rose replied.

"What about?"

"I want to ask him something," Rose said simply. She gazed past the woman and saw a parlor door that opened to the church. A tiny wooden casket stood there almost as small as a box that held notions.

"Ain't here," came her terse reply. She slammed the door in Rose's face.

"Fine!" said Rose heatedly through the door. "I'll just find the sheriff instead and ask him why a man has been hanged here and his body is just left swinging in the wind—especially since there's been no news of a trial or even a conviction. This will make a fine read in my father's newspaper–"

The door flew open and a tall thin wizened man stood there. "Ah, the reverend, I presume?" she asked.

He thundered at her, "And afterward Joshua smote them, and slew them, and hanged them on five trees—and they were hanging on the trees until the evening. Joshua ten, verse twenty-six."

He swung his fist into her face, and Rose crumpled on the porch planks, blood flowing from the corner of her mouth to match the red color of her skirt.

When she awakened, with a monumental aching head and aching jaw, Rose discovered she was behind bars. A green-eyed, black-haired man sat beside her on the bunk, bathing her head with a cloth dipped in cool water.

"I'm Ethan Ridgefield," he said, "Sheriff."

"IF YOU'RE THE sheriff, why am I in jail?" she asked defiantly, sitting up. She sniffed as the smell of fresh coffee brewing filled the jail.

"Because I want to tell you a story," came the casual reply.

"I know you, Miss O'Mallie. I've seen you in Vainglory when I ride that way, working at your father's newspaper. I've even read your stories—'

"You mean my *father's* stories," she said.

He grinned. He was a handsome, long-limbed man.

"All right, we can say it that way. Your, uh, your father's stories, can be very crusading—underdogs, lost dogs, that kind of thing. Burning to set the scheme of things right. I know when somebody's thirsty for justice. And I know when someone is... well, fair."

"You have a sweet way of talking, Sheriff, around what I'm sure has been a lynching," said Rose defiantly. "How long are you going to keep me here, or will you lynch me too to keep me from writing, um, my father, I mean, from writing about what I've seen here?"

"Do you know Hugh McPyle, the man hanging from the tree?" he asked, leaving her alone in the cell with the door opened. He walked to a pot-bellied stove in the corner upon which sat a coffee pot.

"The name seems familiar."

***

RIDGEFIELD POURED TWO cups of coffee from a stippled pot and brought one back to Rose. She gulped the strong black brew, and her head cleared a little. He sat in a chair across from her, and fixed intense green eyes on her that never left her face.

"Hugh McPyle was a murderer, and pardon me, ma'am, a rapist," he said, "who scared any witnesses from testifying against him, and he rode free as the wind because of it. He's been away for a long time, but yesterday he came back. I wasn't here. In fact, I was in Vainglory at Sam Ridgefield's, my cousin. You know, from Sam's study, where he and I play chess, I can see you working sometimes, writing away. Yesterday, you wore a dark blue sweater, high-necked, like the kind the fishermen wear up North. You have an ugly mutt of a dog, with the worst underbite—"

"I'm not here for you to insult my dog," she said tersely. "Are you going to arrest that Bible-thumping hypocrite that slugged me? Because I want to press charges."

"Hear me out first, Miss O'Mallie, and let me tell you what happened," he said.

TAKING A SIP of coffee, Ridgefield leaned back in his chair and told her what happened.

It was a cold November day, in this year of Our Lord 1897. Alice's baby girl, Annie, had been cranky, sick, and colicky. Alice had come into town to see the doctor, and before they faced the cold drive home in an open wagon, she needed hot coffee from the café. She was sitting at a table against a red brick wall, dandling her baby, sipping her coffee, tired from sleepless nights brought on by a crying child and worry. Annie was finally asleep when Hugh McPyle stomped in, took a seat at a table and banged with his fist for immediate service. Annie awakened and began to cry with a cranky roar that continued for some time. Alice tried to quiet her, shooting disapproving looks at that strange man for being so loud. He stared back at her and came to her table.

"Ma'am," he said politely, tipping his hat at her, "I'm sorry I awakened the child. Please give her to me and I will calm her."

Alice, surprised at his courtesy, remembering how the feel of her husband's arms could calm the child, handed Annie to McPyle. He grinned in her face, took the infant by the feet, and swung her head straight into the brick wall.

"There," he said with a chuckle. "I've quieted her."

MCPYLE MADE THE mistake of lingering too long to laugh at his handiwork, the dead baby in the once pink blanket now stained blood-red and her screaming mother reaching for her little body. The townspeople heard Alice's shrill cries from the street and came rushing in, blocking his exit to the street. McPyle's attempt to exit the back door was stymied by a waitress with a skillet who beamed him and the burly cook who held a meat cleaver to his throat. He was dragged out into the street and wrapped in ropes as the roaring crowd and the dust they kicked up encircled him.

And Hugh McPyle, that fierce outlaw brave enough to kill babies, rape women, and terrify witnesses himself grew terrified. He sank to his knees and begged for mercy as tears streamed down his face, but the townspeople were, at that point in time, fresh out.

Six minutes later a horse dragged him to the tree on the barren hill, and as the white steeple of the church looked silently on, his screams and cries rose over the snarl of the mob. Thirty seconds later, he swung in the wind with a crooked neck.

Ridgefield finished his story and looked at Rose, who returned to him a horrified gaze. Wiping fiercely at the tears coursing down her face, she remembered the tiny casket in the church.

Their eyes met and he read her down to her soul.

"NOW, MISS O'MALLIE, was there a lynching out here yesterday?" he asked.

"You're the law here, you're going to let this slide?" Rose asked, somewhat half-heartedly, a monumental knot in her stomach joining the monumental headache. "You're making me part of a crime—"

"Given the circumstances, ma'am, in my absence, the people of this town did nothing more than use self-defense against a vicious criminal. I hope you'll see it that way as well," came the quiet reply.

In a moment, Ridgefield took her arm, and to her surprise, escorted her out to the street. As they passed his desk, Rose saw a copy of *The Adventures of Huckleberry Finn* on his desk.

His green eyes held hers. "Do you like Twain, Miss O'Mallie?"

She nodded.

"I wanted to read a certain passage from it this morning," he said, pointing. "It's my favorite book."

"Mine, too," she said in a whisper. "What passage do you mean?"

HE PAUSED FOR only a second. "The one where Huck decides he'll go to hell before he turns Jim in, as is expected of him."

Whittaker was waiting for her there in the street, as was the minister, and a young couple with dazed, haunted eyes. The knot in Rose's stomach grew larger and the lump in her throat ached.

"Annie was my granddaughter," the minister said. "These are my daughter and son-in-law."

Speechless, they stared at one another for a moment and then she turned to mount her horse. But Ridgefield, to her surprise, lifted her into her saddle. He tipped his hat and said nothing as he silently watched her ride away down the windy, dusty street.

Rose and Whittaker made it back to Vainglory in a sunset with gold and black colors as conflicted as she.

When she entered the two-story building that was both home to her family and the newspaper, she covered her snoring father with a throw as he slept in his office chair, hugged and fed Hardtack, her pot-bellied, bow-legged dog. The windows where her writing table sat, marked where the end of town and where the prairie road, now darkening to purple, began.

Rose lit a hearth fire. Hardtack liked to stretch there after a meal. She sank to the floor beside him staring into the flames.

She knew she was sitting on a whale of a story. It was explosive, involving a murder, and a conspiracy that had the express blessings of the local clergy and law enforcement. The Eastern papers, hungry for any evidence that would report on the savagery of the territory anywhere west of the Mississippi, would lick their chops over this one.

For the next two hours she sat at the wooden table trying to scribble in the golden glow of kerosene light. She was a writer, even if everything she wrote bore her father's byline. Resolute to report what had happened in the neighboring town, her pen kept lagging, and she stared into space. The horror of the baby's death and the grief of the parents held her in a black thrall like funeral garments. But she felt no horror, no indignation remembering the corpse dancing in the wind. Publish this story, and she would destroy an entire town, the life of the minister—and Ridgefield.

Rose slammed down her pen and walked to the bookcase. Reaching upward, she withdrew, *The Adventures of Huckleberry Finn.* Thumbing through the pages, she found the passage about Huck's moral dilemma to turn in Jim—or not.

"'All right then,'" she read out loud, "'I'll go to hell.'"

And she ripped her story to shreds.

—Born in New Orleans, Frois wrote the "Around Louisiana" section for Louisiana Life *magazine from 2002-2017 and has contributed to* The New Orleans Times-Picayune, Southern Living Magazine, Angels on Earth Magazine, New Orleans Magazine, Old House Journal, Gambit Weekly, *and* Country Roads.

She is author of two Louisiana history books: Louisianians All *and* Flags of Louisiana. *and she co-edited and compiled three editions of the* Louisiana Almanac.

INCIDENT OUTSIDE DEADWOOD

RICK SAPP

JAKE LAY THE rifle across the lip of the rock and wiped sweat from his eyes. His eyesight was not as good as the kid's, and his hands were not as steady, but the kid was dead and Jake couldn't save him. Now Jake was alone.

He did not dare lift his head too high to look for the Indians. And as he squirmed to make himself a smaller target, dirt and pebbles worked their way down into his drawers and boots so that, all in all, he was as uncomfortable as he was thirsty and frightful. And he was frightful.

The kid. Jake barely recalled his name. Buck or Chuck or something. From Kansas, he'd said. Maybe sixteen years old. Maybe not even that old.

Jake had just wanted a partner, not a problem. "There's gold up there, kid. All we gotta do is reach down and pick it up and we'll be rich."

He had pointed vaguely "up there," toward the hills between Deadwood and Lead, toward the place the Homestead Company had staked out its claim. "Up there" meant west into the heart of the Black Hills. What these people called Pahá Sápa or some such was what he'd heard. These Indians. These damn Indians. Damn savages. Cut a man's throat just for fun.

The kid laughed and said, "The only good Indian is a dead Indian."

This boy, with all the heedless vanity and innocence of youth. 'Course that was before and what did it matter now? Now, the kid was dead, and Jake was alone, and he was going to die too, and he knew it.

So why didn't they come on? Get it over with? It was the waiting, the not knowing that'd kill a man before a bullet or an arrow or a hatchet.

Besides, Jake only had one or two .45 Government rounds left for his single-shot Sharps. If he carried a shotgun he'd've been better off, he thought. The rifle felt good in his hands though, felt right, even if he never could hit nothing with it. Maybe use it for a club when he ran out of bullets.

Jake didn't believe he'd hit any of 'em, them Indians. Could be he scared 'em a little bit. It hadn't been enough to save the kid, though. But, the kid was dead, and Jake had better figure something out right quick, or he'd be a goner as well.

So Jake lay there, in the rocks of the hillside, in the sun, broiling like one of the steaks the woman labored over before the smallpox came—and the bank—and ruined everything back in Minnesota. Now he envied her, sort of, though the sickness had been terrible, her skin blistering and slithering away as she writhed on the blanket and begged him for help he couldn't give, and then died. And he couldn't do nothing about it, couldn't save her and he felt shameful.

But he couldn't think of her now, the woman. Her suffering was done. Better not think of nothing else but these savages, because he couldn't see 'em and that's when it was bad. The not seeing, not knowing. He was sure they'd watched him run though, and he knew they wouldn't stop 'til they killed him.

Where are you, damn you?

Slow as a spider spinning its web, Jake tilted his head above the top of the rock, but spied no movement—least none he could make out—and so he lifted himself just a little bit higher and then a little more.

As he squinted his eyes and stared left and then right, a trickle of stones and sand tumbled down him. Jake spun and lifted the rifle and pulled the trigger. He acted from reflex. Not an aimed shot, but an instinct, as if he'd grabbed for a flash of gold in a fast moving stream.

In his niche in the rocks, the roar of the big cartridge's burning powder was deafening. His eyes smarted and his ears rang, but there was nothing, no one.

Then, more rocks fell.

Testing me, he thought. Figuring out exactly where I am. He squirmed back and down tight in the crevice and wiped his tired eyes and tried, without success, to control his breathing. He felt dry as a gnawed bone but didn't dare lay the rifle aside and pick up his canteen.

Minutes passed. What seemed hours and Jake was desperate for a drink of water and the sun poured down directly on him and finally he couldn't wait any longer. His legs and back felt like the side of an old barn—warped with age and misery—and he knew they were waiting, up there somewhere, taking their time, though he couldn't figure why.

When night came the stealthy devils would sneak up and slit his throat... or worse. They might just scalp him and leave him, and he'd wish he was dead. Then he'd see the woman again, if any of her prayers came to pass. She believed they would. But Jake didn't know if that was true and wasn't ready to find out. Still, he couldn't just sit in the dirt and wait. The kid's body lay out there in the sun, baked stiff like a slice of bacon on a hot griddle. He didn't want to imagine how they'd desecrated it, and what they'd do to him.

He only had one bullet left and his knife. So Jake resolved to make a run for it. It was miles back to the Deadwood road, but what choice did he have really? Since the rivulet of rock and sand had slid down the slope it must of been—maybe an hour? And of course it might of been a deer or a rabbit or something, but Lord God it was hot.

Jake scraped his feet underneath, held the rifle out to the side, began to push up... and that's right when he saw the Indian. Too late, felt a terrible stab from an arrow through his arm pinning it to his side, and Jake lifted the rifle with one hand and fired blind.

The pain hit him like a rushing one-horn bull, and he fell back hard against the rock, crumpled into the crack and twisted the arm with the arrow. The arrow tore out of his chest, and Jake screamed. He reached across his body to pull his knife and felt blood running down his side.

Come and get me, you sons of bitches!

But nothing happened. Where'd that Indian gone to? Where was he?

Jake rolled to his right and saw a leg, exactly one. A man's leg, twisted at a terrible angle. As Jake watched, the man pushed upward, drew a knife and motioned as if he would surely cut him.

There must be more of 'em, Jake reasoned, not just this one man. He wouldn't be alone, would he? When they killed the kid there were several. Where'd they go?

"Where's your friends?" Jake taunted the man. "Where they gone? They run off and left you, that's what. Forgot all about you."

The Indian grunted something in reply, but Jake didn't understand. When he shifted his weight, the arrowhead cut and gouged his side, and Jake closed his eyes and groaned. He thought about trying to pull the arrow out. Knew he couldn't. He'd heard of men who done that and then bled to death—and he was already bleeding down his shirt and into his trousers. He'd have to break the arrow shaft off first, but just to touch it made him gag, made his head throb mightily.

The Indian didn't move and Jake could see that the twisted leg had to be broken, and broke bad. Awful painful, he figured. He won't be goin' nowhere too quick. So Jake leaned back against the rock again and took a deep breath.

He weren't too many miles off the road, up a canyon between Deadwood and Lead. Maybe somebody heard the shooting. They'd notice the kid's body and go fetch the sheriff. Maybe somebody would come.

The Indian was moving now. Slow and careful. Could be trying to roll over, get his good leg under him. Crawl over here and finish me off. But Jake could tell from the man's jerky movements and the anguish visible in his face that the leg hurt miserable bad.

Must hurt like hell. Good! You filthy Indian bastard.

He wondered if it was the fall or his bullet had caused the bad leg. Whatever. Didn't much matter. Otherwise Jake'd already be dead.

The two men lay in the dirt and rocks and held their knives and glared at each other while the sun dipped toward the hills.

The night would be cold and Jake was so thirsty he could swallow his tongue. The canteen strap lay just out a ways and he leaned and reached and gave a yelp when the steel arrowhead cut into him, but with his good arm he grabbed the strap and drew the canteen toward him.

Oh, good Lord! The water was cool and he swallowed and swallowed again, and for the briefest moment felt better and he replaced the canteen cap and began to think of ways to get out of his predicament. Nothing especially occurred to him because every movement now was an agony. He so much as wiggled a toe and a flood of hot iron washed through him, pain like the Devil hisself had got him with a pitchfork.

Jake lay the canteen aside, saw the Indian squirm and snatched up his knife. "Come get me, you son of a bitch," he growled and swished the knife like he was gutting a chicken.

But the Indian only watched as Jake drank from the canteen again. Indeed, the Indian had laid his knife aside and appeared to be in torment trying—and failing—to straighten his leg.

Son of a bitch is hurt as bad as me, Jake realized. Maybe worse. And then, for some unknown reason, he put the canteen to his lips and, with the cap still in place, pretended to drink. The Indian watched, never taking his eyes away.

Damn if he ain't thirsty too. And he'll be a-freezin tonight like me, 'less his buddies come back. Jake stared at the Indian's leather leggings and breechcloth. The man wore a plaid shirt that he might have traded for or might have stolen, but it was twisted up beneath a bone breastplate.

The Indian moaned and seemed to give up, replaced the knife in its beaded sheath and leaned back into the rocks.

And then, Jake never understood why, although the cooling day and the appearance of the first bright star in the east occurred to him later, he picked up a stone and knocked it against the canteen's tin side. Or perhaps it was the wrenching memory of his wife, the eternal ache and loneliness of life without her, because now he was alone, truly alone, and he felt it. So here was this Indian, this savage who'd tried to kill him, and he was also alone.

The Indian immediately looked up and Jake, his hand shaking, held the canteen out to him.

At first, the man only looked away. Simple as Jake was, he read doubt, fear, disdain, even desperation in the squinched face. Then, the Indian reached out. Not far enough, and Jake heard a muffled sob. The man's face contorted in pain. Jake tightened the cap and swung the canteen once, twice, and flung it toward the Indian. The man immediately took a drink. His head rocked back with a fleeting aura of relief, and Jake sheathed his knife.

"What now, you son of a bitch?" It was more an utterance of despair than a challenge.

The Indian looked quizzically at the white man, his head slightly to the side. "Bitch. Dog."

"Oh, my Lord, you speak American!"

"Little English."

Sunshine highlighted the far hills. Stringy gray clouds raced overhead, throwing the two men into alternate sun and shadow. Jake felt cold come on like the icy hand of death. He began to shudder.

Gotta do something pretty quick, or I'm gonna die here. He's gonna die, too, being alone and all. Looks like his friends done up and left him for dead.

Then the Indian swung the canteen back by its strap, and this surprised Jake who assumed the man would drink it all.

Well, I ain't gonna lie here and just wait to bleed out. I gotta get help and so does he. Let's see how this'll work. Jake loosened one end of the long canteen strap and wrapped it once around his hand.

"Here, Chief." He again tossed the canteen toward the Indian. "Pull me up." Jake gestured with his hand. Might the Indian have understood?

Instead, the Indian brushed the canteen aside and drew his knife.

Well, what the heck! We ain't got time for that. Jake, a practical man, realized the Indian, whose age he could not fathom, but who did not appear to be old, was afraid of him.

And so, in a moment of inspiration, Jake reached for his rifle and slid it across the dirt. The Indian hesitated and then pulled it toward him, opened the receiver and saw that it was empty.

He laid it aside.

"Now, you son of a bitch, grab that strap and pull," Jake said, tugging at the leather canteen strap. The man only stared at him.

He don't trust me. Even now, after giving him water.

So Jake pulled the canteen back, took a sip and again tossed it to the Indian. He pointed to the arrow in his arm and made a motion with his good hand as if to break the wooden shaft and pull the arrow out of his arm. Finally, the Indian seemed to appreciate Jake's idea and took the canteen strap in his hands.

Jake struggled to his knees. In spite of the evening cold, he began to sweat. The arrow shaft brushed against the boulder which, only moments earlier had saved him from certain death, and caused a moment of blinding pain. He closed his eyes and clenched his teeth to keep from passing out.

Jake moved toward the Indian but the man took out his knife, an instrument Jake was certain he knew how to use.

"Break," he said, again pointing to the arrow, "break."

"Break." The Indian repeated the word, still holding the knife.

Jake was losing blood. To live another day he would have to trust this other man. But the woman had trusted him when Jake said he wanted to move west onto the prairie and the kid had trusted him when he said he wanted to pan for gold and where had that got 'em? But now he pointed to the man's leg and to the rifle. "Fix," he said, not knowing how much the man would understand. "Splint. Fix leg." He gestured with his good arm and saw incomprehension in the brown face, so he drew his knife, dropped it into the dust, and kicked it toward the prostrate warrior.

"Help leg," he said, and pointed, then patted his own leg. He could cut the canteen strap and tie the broken leg to the rigid rifle stock and barrel, there being no trees within reach, though he wished for a stout pine branch. 'Course, he might as well wish for the sheriff and a posse to come thundering down the canyon and rescue him.

At last, the Indian seemed to comprehend and returned his knife to its sheath. He nudged Jake's knife back toward Jake with his good leg, but even that effort caused him to contort in pain. Nevertheless, he motioned Jake to come to him.

Jake hunched forward protectively, nervous, each motion a stabbing torment until at last he knelt down beside the Indian.

"You stink," he said and instantly regretted the unnecessary comment. His good hand felt toward the knife.

"You stink," the Indian replied in a voice thin with fear and pain and then signed for Jake to come closer.

There was no going back now. If the Indian was going to kill him, this would be the moment. Jake knelt down, careful of the broken leg.

The Indian studied the arrow. "Hurt," he said and Jake nodded. "Much hurt."

Jake inclined forward, closed his eyes, and in two swift motions the Indian snapped the wooden arrow shaft and yanked it out of Jake's arm.

When Jake awakened it was almost dark. His shirt and trousers were stiff with blood. Wishing for quiet and sleep but searching for strength, he unharnessed his suspenders and tore his bloody shirt away. He motioned to the Indian, who lay, watchfully, almost beneath him.

"Wrap," he said and pantomimed what he wanted done. The Indian tied the shirt around Jake's bleeding wound, then pointed to his own leg.

Night was coming fast, and Jake felt weak as a baby, but this was the bargain, the agreement, and so it was necessary. And although he was a poor man and practically unlettered, Jake was a man of his word. He'd made bargains before, with the woman and with the kid, but they were both gone, and Jake was alone with his conscience. He had been helpless to prevent their deaths, but when he thought of them, he felt an anvil drop into his heart.

Jake studied the fallen man and said, "Hurt, chief."

Remarkably, the man seemed to smile, or grimace, and again said, "No chief. Much hurt."

When it was over, and the Indian had come to, for the movement and strapping the broken leg to the rifle must have been terrible almost beyond Jake's imagining, Jake leaned down and the two shared the last of the water.

"We go." Jake motioned, and the Indian put out his arm.

"We go."

Jake forever remembered the next few minutes as the most exhausting of his life. That and burying his wife back east, deep under the prairie sod, deep under their unrealized dreams.

The night was cold, and Jake was not sure he could move, but overhead, in the early dark whirled an almost unimaginable universe of stars. There'd be frost in the morning. In his condition a killing frost.

The two men had little choice but to limp together down the uneven slope in the direction of the kid's body. The Indian one-legged and awkward with an arm around Jake's good side.

At the slope's end, Jake collapsed. The Indian tumbled and both men screamed and fainted.

Right about then Jake heard the sound of horses. Nah, he thought, not after all this, and his thoughts wandered and a heavy weight twisted on top of him, taking his breath away.

Jake thought about his hair. It wasn't much hair and was no longer brown, but it was his and he figured, damn, there goes my scalp. And that made him tremble with fear. He would miss his hair, and he wondered how much it was going to hurt and whether they would torture him before they murdered him. He decided they probably would.

The last thing Jake remembered was hearing shouting that he couldn't understand and then the words, "No! Friend."

When Jake woke the day was bright and hard as a new axe handle. The sunshine surprised him, but it was warm on his face and with his good arm and hand he felt for his hair.

Jake opened his eyes and found that he was wrapped in a blanket. The ground was hard, bitter, but he was alive and he heard a grunt and saw an Indian—not the man with the broken leg, but a younger man—squatting nearby.

The Indian pushed Jake's canteen forward with his foot and stood up. Behind this man lay the body of the kid, but the Indian ignored it and pointed to a pony.

"Go," he said and again pointed.

Jake struggled to his feet, feeling the earth spin and the ground shake, and willed himself not to faint. He felt for his hair and knew he was alive, but without strength to pull himself onto a pony. A staggering step. Another step.

"Go. Now."

Jake led the pony to a tumble of rocks, slithered up and across its back and watched the Indian. The man had not moved, and Jake said, "Thank you." And turned the pony toward Deadwood.

—Rick Sapp is a freelance writer who now lives in the Appalachian Mountains of North Georgia. His recent past includes years in Colorado and New Mexico and one day he hopes to slip on his black Stetson to see those high, dry mountains and wide blue skies once again.

A CRACK IN THE ICE SKIN

PAUL A. J. LEWIS

I CAN'T RECALL every step that led me to my current predicament. When I looked back upon the events that had transpired, trying to retrace exactly how I wound up with such a cruel thirst for blood and chaos, the logic in the sequence became obscured in a dense fog of hatred and violence.

The day was heading to evening, and I lay prone on a blanket of snow atop a hill overlooking Old Petersen's cabin and partially hidden amongst a stand of quaking aspen trees. My long gun remained trained on the cabin's closed door.

It had been a long winter. Long and cruel. The loss I had felt as it began, with the needless deaths of my wife and infant son, had been driven home by the icy winds and heavy snowfall. These became kin to an expression of the sudden coldness that had enveloped my heart during that frozen season. The subzero temperatures and the thick snow on the ground had lasted so long that it felt like my boots hadn't been dry in a decade or more. It amplified the distance in time between my present state as a bestial creature driven by a ferocious need for revenge and my prior existence as a civilized family man and a lawyer.

It was whilst working in the law offices back east that I had met Milly, my wife and the mother of my son. That was long before my family had been slaughtered, cruelly and unnecessarily, by the Duchamp gang.

———————✦———————

MY MEMORIES WERE overshadowed with a deep sense of guilt, for it was I who had dragged Milly to Colorado. She had been reluctant to come, concerned about upending our lives and raising Josiah in an unfamiliar environment, one so different from that which we both knew. But I had been confident that we could make our riches in Colorado and badgered Milly to acquiesce to my demands.

When both of her parents died of consumption within a year of one another, I managed to convince Milly that the air in Colorado would be better for Josiah. I told her that living away from the city would improve our lives, that it would make us happier.

I was so incredibly, desperately wrong.

The memory of my wife—picturing her smile, her hair blowing in the wind and framing her delicate features—thawed the coldness in my heart. But remembering Milly's death, and what her killers did to her, caused that same organ to freeze over and shatter into a thousand pieces. I don't know whether the torture they inflicted on Milly took place before or after those same men put a bullet in the brain of our two-year-old son. I dread to think of him as a passive witness to their intolerable cruelty.

I had sworn to avenge my wife and child. Every night since Milly had been killed, I heard her voice crying out for vengeance—for herself, but also for our son whose life was cut short before it had even begun.

I had been in town at the time buying supplies for the winter, and I heard from an old timer that the Duchamp gang had been seen heading toward our home. The Duchamps had a bad reputation, and something told me to hurry back to my wife and child.

I had no idea how they had found out about the small amount of gold Milly and I had brought with us from back east. It represented everything we had worked and saved for. But then, I was not completely certain that the gold was the reason why they came to our small home. Maybe they just wanted chaos, to satiate their bloodlust. Maybe they came because they knew Milly was alone. Or maybe they simply stumbled across our plot of land on their way to somewhere else, and there was no planning in their actions whatsoever.

Since then, six men had died. Six men who deserved their deaths. I wished to match the savage cruelty they had inflicted on Milly, but was unable to…. Three had died swift deaths, or as swift as a bullet to the brain or the heart would allow. I left one to die in the snow and ice—a shot to the gut leaving the ground beneath him stained with his own blood. Forty miles from nowhere and without a horse, his death was certain and would have been unpleasant. I didn't need to watch him expire and, as I rode away, took pleasure in his pleas for mercy and his cries for me to put him out of his misery. I'm not ashamed to say that I laughed at him as he pleaded. Two more had died slowly, protractedly. A knife had made their deaths intimate, and I had relished their suffering.

I knew I was becoming a monster…. But still….

But still, their deaths were less cruel than Milly's, and try as I might, I could dispatch the Duchamp gang but perhaps never feel like my vengeance was entirely complete. Regardless, I took an almost professional delight in eradicating them, the way one might feel pride in destroying a nest of rats or vipers.

I hope you are watching me, Milly, and witnessing my revenge in your name.

———◆———

I HAD NO reason to believe the Duchamp brothers had left Old Petersen's cabin. I was pretty sure that, even considering I was near-as-dammit 250 yards away, I had heard both of their horses whinny in Petersen's barn, which was closer to me than the cabin. The wind, travelling in my direction, had helped carry that sound to my elevated position on the hilltop.

The distance didn't concern me. I had high winds to contend with, but I trusted my accuracy, and I trusted my Sharps rifle even more. I had been in the First Battalion New York Sharpshooters during the war, and the rifle—my service weapon—had come with me when Milly and I moved to Colorado.

The rifle had served me well during that conflict, but killing men in war felt different. It felt essential, a matter of life and death. By contrast, killing the members of the Duchamp gang had a flavor all of its own, and in its brutal necessity, it had become almost pleasurable. After the war, I had put my Sharps away. I hadn't even hoped that I would never have to use it again, simply because I foresaw no situation in which its use would be needed. Yet still, I maintained the weapon, keeping it lubricated and in good shape—more out of habit than anything else.

I half-cocked my Sharps and yanked its lever, lowering the breech block, before loading the rifle with a paper cartridge and raising the breech again. I tipped some powder onto the nipple, then put my firing cap in place.

I checked my range and judged the weather, making adjustments to my aim.

Then I waited.

I DIDN'T HAVE to wait too long. When I had killed the last member of the Duchamp gang—leaving just the Duchamp brothers themselves, I had taken from his dead horse a buffalo hide. I was laying on this now. It provided some insulation from the freezing bed of snow beneath me, but with the wind and temperature being what it was, my whole body had begun to feel damp. The cold wetness of the air and the ground radiated into and through me.

My thick leather gloves protected my hands from the cold, but I had cut away the trigger finger of the glove on the right hand so that I could better fire my rifle, and my index finger was becoming numb.

When I saw the door of Old Petersen's cabin begin to open, I breathed a sigh of relief. Soon it would all be over.

I took a half-breath into my lungs and steadied my rifle.

The door opened fully. A figure, wearing a black gambler hat, stepped out of its black depths and into the sight of my rifle. I fired. The shot rang out a fraction of a second before I saw the gambler hat explode in a shower of red, blood and brain matter spattering the wall behind it. The figure crumpled to the floor, seemingly in slow-motion, before slowly rolling onto its side and gasping its last breath.

That was when I realised I had shot Old Petersen and not one of the Duchamps. I had assumed Old Petersen to be dead or trussed up inside the cabin, but the Duchamps had neither killed nor restrained him. I could only assume he had either helped the Duchamps willingly, or they had deceived him, and he was unaware of their savage temperament and criminal proclivities.

As the old man expired, his head thrown back and his chest rising with sharp gasps, a red stain slowly spread beneath him staining the snow. The door to the cabin swung further open.

"You just unleashed hell!" A rage-filled voice yelled from inside.

A shot whistled from the cabin, and fifty yards in front of me, snow burst into the air as the round hit the dirt. Then another shot fired out... and another, both striking the snow-covered ground a good three or four dozen yards ahead of my position. Mikey, the youngest of the two Duchamp brothers, emerged in the doorway holding a repeating rifle. Its range and accuracy was no match for my Sharps.

I took this time to reload my rifle, confident that the chances of being hit with a round from Mikey Duchamp's repeating rifle were next to nought.

I took aim and fired again, but the cold must have made my Sharps— or maybe my aim—a little sluggish. The bullet dropped, striking Mikey in his right leg just above his kneecap.

Mikey fell to the floor, growling in pain like a wounded animal. He held onto the rifle. Then Pete Duchamp appeared in the doorway dragging Mikey into the cabin. Pete was a giant of a man and towered over his injured brother. Both of them quickly disappeared into the darkness of the cabin's interior.

I reloaded the Sharps and waited, patient-like, with my sights trained on the cabin door.

Suddenly, another shot rang out. This one had a different timbre to it, and behind me I heard my horse whinny sharply before slumping to the ground.

Damn it! No one had come through the cabin door. Where had the shot come from?

I turned my attention to the sides of the cabin, and saw—peeking around the far corner—Pete Duchamp taking aim with a rifle. Only this wasn't the repeating rifle that Mikey had been using. It looked like a long gun to rival my Sharps.

I swung my Sharps toward Pete and took quick aim at him before pulling the trigger. Nothing. A misfire.

Another shot from the direction of the cabin rang out. This time it struck the ground within feet of me.

I didn't have time to clear the misfire and reload my rifle. I was a sitting duck.

Within seconds, I was on my feet, ducking low, and running. I ran past my horse, and could only glance at it as it lay in the deep snow, gasping. Meeting the cold air, my horse's final breaths formed a misty cloud at its nostrils. It seemed Pete Duchamp's round had hit the horse in the chest, probably tearing through one of its lungs and maybe striking its heart.

"I'm comin' for you, boy," Pete Duchamp said from behind me. "You better ready your soul!"

I took it on the arches, as swiftly as I could, running through the trees. The bare branches wouldn't offer much cover, if they offered any at all. Conscious of how deep the snow was, it would make my passage through the trees easy to trace. But I had no shelter, nowhere to hide, and fled blindly.

Then I recalled the large lake nearby. There might be shelter there, I reasoned.

As I ran through the snowdrifts, each step became more sluggish. The cold air was sharp on my face and in my lungs. It was dusk, and I could only hope that the failing light would aid me, concealing my escape. Behind me, I could hear the cracking of the trees, and I imagined Pete Duchamp in pursuit, having gathered his horse from the stable and tracking my steps. Once or twice, I thought I heard—or imagined—the sharp breathing and snorting of Pete's horse too close for comfort.

NIGHT HAD BEGUN to fall. The snow was falling heavier now. So heavy, in fact, that visibility was very low. I could only hope that the fresh snowfall had obscured my tracks making it difficult, or perhaps impossible, for Pete to track me.

I'd made it through the trees and to the shore of the lake, finding some shelter in a ramshackle wooden structure that, I assumed, had been used as a hut by men who fished at the lake.

With my back against the wall of the shelter, I held in my right hand my Colt 1860—another souvenir from the war.

I remained silent but could hear my own heavy heartbeat. Beyond the shelter, in the trees that bordered the lake, I heard the snow shift and branches crack under its weight. Every now and then, I would hear the hoot of an owl which I assumed nested nearby.

I looked out across the frozen expanse of the lake. It seemed endless on the left and right, and I estimated that it was perhaps a thousand yards across. Though it was obscured from me by the falling snow, I knew that on the other side of the bank was another thick treeline. I wondered if I could make it across the lake. There was no way around it.

Then my thoughts returned once more to my beautiful wife and the moment when I had found the bodies of Milly and our son. My wife's body broken beyond imagination and our child lifeless and frozen. I washed both bodies before spending several hours digging their shared grave. The frost hadn't fully settled at that point, so the ground still responded to the shovel. I buried Milly and Josiah together, as I knew they would have wished me to, and then said a prayer for my wife to take care of our son in the next life and wait for me there.

During that time, I planned my revenge. I knew the direction in which the Duchamps had been heading. The tracks from their mounts made this all too evident. From there, I only had to find the first member of the gang and make him talk. I followed a train of evidence that, in their arrogance, the Duchamp brothers had failed to conceal.

MY REVERIE WAS interrupted by a voice that roared from within the treeline.

"I'm here for you now." Pete's voice roared. "You'll pay for what you did to my brother... in this life *and* the next!"

I steadied myself, closing my eyes for a fraction of a second and feeling the heat of my hatred for Pete Duchamp. I resisted the urge to shout back at him, to engage him in dialogue. There were no words for what I had to do. My need for revenge could only be expressed through action.

I didn't have my long gun. Pete was in the treeline somewhere, too far for an accurate shot with my Colt. I'd have to lure him closer in order to get a shot at him.

I peered around the shelter, trying to gauge where Pete was.

A shot rang out from the treeline, hitting the wooden shelter.

I withdrew behind it. I judged the shelter to be directly between me and Pete, otherwise he would have fired at me from another angle.

"You'll have to come down, Pete Duchamp!" I yelled. "You'll have to come down here and face me so I can put you down like the beast that you are!"

Another shot rang out, and the bullet hit the snow about four feet in front of me.

The lake was frozen, or perhaps only the surface of the lake was frozen. It was difficult to ascertain. The ice skin was covered in such a thick layer of snow, and visibility was limited so much by the heavy snowfall that it was difficult to tell at first glance where the shore ended and the lake began.

I resolved myself to step on the lake, keeping the wooden shelter between me and where I judged Pete Duchamp to be.

Upon stepping onto the snow and ice, my footsteps had a different resonance—both in sensation and the sound they made. The thick bed of snow upon the ice skin offered some traction, which meant that I could walk across the frozen lake with relative ease.

I headed across the ice, as quickly as I could, praying the lake was frozen enough to ensure my safe passage across it.

The snowfall became heavier.

"I see you!" Pete said from somewhere behind me. I didn't doubt him.

The wind tore at my face and clothing as I headed across the lake. Owing to the pounding snowfall, my vision was limited to less than twenty feet. Behind me, I heard the heavy, echoing steps of Pete's horse as its hooves hit the thick ice underneath the bed of snow. The steps were heavy and slow. I reasoned that Pete must be edging his horse carefully across the ice—either confident that the ice could support its weight or so driven by rage that he didn't care.

I had got maybe a hundred yards across the lake when I heard Pete's voice, lower this time.

"Turn around," he said with a growl. "I want to see your face as you die."

I hesitated.

"Turn around, I said." The demand added a bitter urgency in his voice.

I slowly turned. My Colt was in my right hand at my side. I made no show of raising it.

Pete was still on horseback. He had the repeating rifle in his right hand and held the reins of his horse in his left.

"Why'd you shoot at us?" Pete said. "I need to know. Afore I take your life, I need you to tell me why you killed my brother."

"You murdered my family." My voice was a cold hiss. "You killed my wife and son." I felt my blood boil and rise.

"Your wife and son, huh?" I could see him processing the information. "Three, four months ago? A cabin about ten miles out of a mining town?"

"That'd be it," I said in a snarl. "Grown faint in your memory, has it?"

"I remember," he said. "I remember that cabin. They was already dead when we got there." He laughed. It was a bitter laugh, not good natured-like. "If you've been trackin' us since then, you been trackin' the wrong folks."

His words made me hesitate. Had I made a terrible mistake? Had this winter been spent on a fool's errand? Had my certainty in the guilt of the Duchamps allowed my wife and son's killers to escape?

Nevertheless, there was a surety in my need to see this man dead. I desired it. I would will it into being.

"Your wife, she looked like she'd been a pretty fine woman when she was alive. But she was already dead as a doornail when we got there." Pete Duchamp paused. I watched as he narrowed his eyes. "I see my words have stung you. We ain't the folks that killed your family. But I'm still gonna kill you, in the name of my kid brother." He hesitated, watching me closely. "Say your prayers."

I had my eye fixed on Pete Duchamp's left hand. He grasped the reins of his horse tighter, a sign that he was readying himself to fire the rifle.

As Pete pulled the trigger, I ducked low and fired my Colt simultaneously. My gun wasn't aimed at Pete but at a patch of the ice between the front hooves of his horse. Ducking low didn't count for much because Pete's repeating rifle misfired anyway. Pete's expression momentarily transformed from anger to confusion, then to rage.

In rapid succession, I fired two, three, four times at the same spot.

There was a moment of quiet that seemed to last for an eternity. Then I heard—and Pete must have heard—the ice skin on the surface of the frozen lake began to crack... subtly at first, and then more aggressively. Pete's horse snorted, the vapor from its nostrils reminding me of a painting I had once seen back east of a mythical dragon breathing fire.

"I guess you got me," Pete Duchamp muttered. He let the repeating rifle fall to the ice and grabbed the horse's reins with both hands. Teasing the reins, he commanded the horse to slowly, steadily step backwards as the ice skin cracked beneath the horse's hooves, jagged lines emanating from the place where my bullets had hit the surface of the frozen lake.

As Pete's dropped rifle landed on the ice, it discharged. The shot echoed in the near-silence.

Pete Duchamp's horse reached the edge of my visibility, gradually fading into the snowstorm. Horse and rider vanished wordlessly, and it seemed possible that they had never been there—as if they were phantoms of my imagination. The ethereal quality of that moment made me question the reality of what had happened.

I thought about Pete's words and wondered about the level of truth within them.

My stomach felt wet when I reached down to my belly. When I held my hand in front of me, I realised it was soaked with blood. It was then I realised I'd been shot in the gut when Pete's rifle had discharged upon hitting the ice.

There was no pain. The freezing cold saw to that. There was just a numbness at the center of me, in the core of myself.

Not caring whether I lived or died, I turned around and headed toward the shore of the lake, uncertain whether or not I would make it.

The snow continued to fall. Everything was white.

—Paul A J Lewis is a writer and lecturer from Lincolnshire in the United Kingdom. His writing encompasses both fiction and non-fiction, the latter focusing on film noir and neo-noir, the Western, and horror cinema. His work has been published in books and magazines including the Film Noir Foundation's publication Noir City, *and he has also produced booklet essays and video essays for DVD/Blu-ray releasing companies.*

Moonlight Wolf by Frederic Remington

THE LAST ODD JOB AT CRIPPLE CREEK

MICHAEL MITCHELL, JR.

IT WAS NEARLY midnight when Rudy Carlos boomed like a cannonball through the front swivel doors into the crowded Copperhead Saloon. A dancehall girl bounced on each of Carlos' arms, cackling at each joke he shouted above the singing and drunken conversation. Carlos parted the packed room like a shark through the waves.

When Benito saw him, his fingers scrambled over the piano keys to finish his song.

"Mister Carlos, may I have a word?" asked Benito. His thick fingers patted down his black hair then twisted his sloping mustache.

Carlos stopped, but his cigar continued puffing like a steam engine. With his plump face, bug eyes, and squished nose, Mr. Carlos reminded Benito of a bulldog in a black top hat.

The tall girl with blonde hair said, "I can play 'Oh! Susanna'," and pounded on the keys, as she and her friend exploded into more laughter.

"What's this?" she asked, picking up a small wooden box next to Benito's sheet music, an image of the Virgin Mary painted on the top. Benito shooed her hands away and slipped the box into his vest pocket.

He cleared his throat and recited the speech that Lucia had helped him practice all week. "Mister Carlos, I've been playing here for a month, every weekend, and I haven't been paid. You said it would be every two weeks."

Carlos' dimpled smile twisted into pursed lips. "The drought's been tough on everyone. You're lucky I keep you on at all. Buck Stevens takes all his players' tips at his place in Colorado Springs. They get ten percent. I don't do that, do I?"

Benito was silent, his fingers pulling at the hairs above his lips. He hadn't practiced a response.

Carlos paused, looking around and wiping his face with a handkerchief. "Where is that old rebel—doesn't he play guitar with you?"

Benito winced. He hated being linked with the pale, rat-faced man with his slick gray hair and crooked smile. Jed Linford drifted into Cripple Creek around the same time Benito and his wife arrived. Most nights, Linford staggered in late with his guitar in one hand and a flask of whiskey in the other. Linford said he needed the extra cash to send to his bedridden cousin in Raleigh, so Carlos let him play.

For a split second, Benito considered telling Carlos what Linford was really up to, but he told a partial truth instead. "He's taking his break in the alley."

"Tell him he'll get paid next week." Carlos playfully smacked one of the dancer's backsides causing another eruption of giggles, and the three swam back into the cloud of tobacco smoke.

Benito pushed through the huddle of men belting Irish tunes and slid up to the bar. He scanned the room for Jeremiah, the barkeep, who was near the front mopping up a puddle of brown vomit. When an old rancher stumbled away, Benito saw the sparkle of copper coins left next to the foam-stained mugs and empty bottles. He hesitated, his hand hovering near the coins.

A bony hand slid beside his and plucked them up.

It was Linford.

"You talk to Carlos? I bet it went just like I said it would," Linford said. The scattering of men around the bar roared with laughter at the latest tales of treasure-filled mines and paid no attention as Linford pocketed the coins.

"Don't bring that in here." Benito nodded toward the canvas sack in Linford's hand.

"Bring what? No one is worried about my dirty long johns." Linford swung the bag over his shoulder alongside his cowhide leather guitar case. During his break, Linford lurked around the horses tied out front, nabbing whatever he could from the drunk patrons' saddlebags and carts.

"Quiet. Here comes Jeremiah," said Linford. "Calm down, you look like you swallowed a scorpion, *amigo.*" He laughed, flashing a smile with a cavern of missing teeth.

"You boys still looking for extra work?" asked Jeremiah, his eyes darting to the drinkers at the bar and around the room. He ran his skinny fingers through his thick white hair and wiped his hands on his stained patchwork apron.

"I'll take anything you got," said Benito. He wished Linford hadn't chosen that moment to appear.

"I'm in." Linford leaned his elbows on the bar. "Right, partner?" Linford turned to Benito and smiled his jack-o'-lantern grin. Benito focused on Jeremiah.

"My brother-in-law, Everett, is up in the hills panning," said Jeremiah. "Needs a supply run. Can't make it up there with my bum leg. Come by my place tomorrow morning at five. I'll have two mules packed up."

"I'll be there," said Benito. Linford nodded with a tip of his gray slouch hat.

"Last call!" Jeremiah shouted. He grabbed the broom and limped toward a table littered with empty mugs.

After their shift, Benito rushed out into the warm night air and hurried toward the Palace Hotel. Linford followed close behind. A few dogs barked as they passed.

"What'd you get, partner?" said Linford.

Benito thought back to the crammed tip jar and scattered coins on the bar. *I promised Father Volpe I'm not doing that anymore.*

Benito recalled the candle-lit room at the parish and Father Volpe's soft voice behind the screen. After his confession, he felt like he was a kid again, floating on his back in the cool water of the acequias running through Santa Fe. *Weightless and free.*

"There wasn't a chance," Benito said, trying to change the topic.

"There's always a chance, partner," said Linford, as he took a swig from his flask. "You just got to know when to strike."

"Mister Carlos came in tonight. He's paying us next week."

Linford nodded and rolled a cigarette. "You believe that, don't you?" Benito was silent.

"Carlos is a rattler in a hog's skin. That's why I got a side business, feeding off his prey," Linford said, tapping the bag on his shoulder.

Benito watched the light of the cigarette fade into black as Linford squeezed between the stacks of empty milk bottles and spoiled cabbage and disappeared into the alley next to Major's General Store.

The next morning, Benito left a note for Lucia then crept out under the starry sky. Their shack behind the Palace Hotel leaned against a horse stable, and Benito heard the mustangs pushing and neighing, anticipating their morning feeding. Lucia would be up soon with Rosita, but Benito didn't want to wake her on a Saturday since she didn't have to be at the hotel until after lunch.

They arrived at the Palace Hotel in Cripple Creek last year, hoping for work in the goldrush town. Lucia kept their baby strapped on her back as she hauled water back and forth to the kitchen and washrooms. When not scrubbing pots, Benito spent his breaks at the lobby's grand piano, their daughter wrapped to his chest. Little Rosita loved the music and slept the whole time. Jeremiah heard him playing one afternoon and recommended him to Mr. Carlos' place for weekends.

A rooster's crowing greeted Benito when he got to Jeremiah's place. Linford wasn't there yet. Benito sat with Jeremiah on the porch for nearly a half hour, watching Jeremiah blow pipe smoke at the dusty moths fluttering near the oil lamps. Linford never showed, so Jeremiah sent Benito off with the mules.

"They won't let you bring up any weapons," Jeremiah said. Benito held out his empty hands.

Jeremiah gave him a square of torn paper. "Here are the directions to the rendezvous point... it's a couple hours away on foot. Signed by me for authenticity." He paused. "Don't tell anybody where you're going."

Directions in hand, Benito led the mules to the outside of town until he saw what townspeople called The Last Shitrow. The half-dozen connected outhouses sat at the base of a series of trails fanning up into the hills. Carved images of animals, vulgar pictures, and people's initials covered the stinking shanties. Benito covered his nose with his handkerchief.

"So which path we headed on?" said a voice behind the outhouses. Benito jumped, his heart sinking when he recognized the slurred speech.

Jed Linford staggered over to Benito. His eyes were red cobwebs, and the deep lines in his tanned face made him look even older than his nearly fifty years. His black pants and gray Confederate jacket melted into the hazy dawn light, but the worn spots on the cowhide guitar case strapped across his back popped out like beacons of light.

"You're late," said Benito, noticing the bedroll and empty whiskey bottles next to the outhouse. The two mules shifted their weight, their floppy ears twitching at the gnats buzzing around their heads.

Linford leaned against the nearest mule and untied a package. A couple of eggs dropped into the rocks, the yolks seeping into the dirt. He held one up, squinting as an orange ray of sunrise lit up the egg's shell like a candle.

"Figured I'd catch you here on the way." He cracked the egg and slurped at the yolk dripping through his dirty fingers.

In the breeze, Benito caught the stench of the sweat dried into Linford's old Confederate jacket, and he took a step back. He'd never seen Linford without that worn gray coat, even in the summer heat.

Benito tugged at the mules' reins to move up the trail. "This is my job now."

Linford's eyes narrowed and stared at Benito like he'd never seen him before. He smiled. "You were gonna scamper up a Shitrow trail without me, partner?"

Linford grabbed for the reins, but Benito pushed him back. Linford pulled down his hat over his eyes and stumbled in close to Benito's ear, so close that Benito could taste the booze from Linford's breath as he spoke.

"You don't want Jeremiah to find out that his good buddy Benito has been pinching tips off his bar. My guess is that Mister Carlos won't appreciate that much either."

Benito wiped the sweat from his forehead and looked down at the town nestled in the morning haze. Lucia didn't know he'd taken the tips to help pay for their board and food last month. He'd put the money back in Jeremiah's tip jars as soon as he had it. He just needed to get it first.

"Fine. Grab a mule. But only I know the way, so you follow me," said Benito.

"Lead on," said Linford.

Benito wanted to punch his jack-o'-lantern grin.

Over the next two hours, they climbed up the rocky trail, the heat creeping over the hills as the sun muscled its way into the center of the pale blue sky. The scorched landscape was silent, except for the rhythmic buzz of the insects in the tall brown grass. Benito clutched his rosary beads and mumbled Hail Marys as they walked. Linford was silent, except for the occasional whistling of some sad *corrido* Benito had taught him.

Benito's mule snorted and dug its hooves into the dirt and pebbles, sending clouds of dust billowing into the dry air.

"Something's got her spooked. Or she's just as tired of your prayers as I am," said Linford, who stopped to roll a cigarette a few feet down the trail behind Benito.

In front of them, a rattlesnake slithered onto the trail, its scaly body curling up into a coiled, hissing threat.

"I've seen these bastards all the time back in Wilmington," said Linford, stepping beside him. "We'd sometimes eat them at our camp when the supply wagons didn't make it through. Ever had rattler meat?"

Linford slid a knife from his belt and crept up to the snake sprawled in front of them, its rattle shaking like a war drum.

"You just got to show it who's boss," said Linford, crouching and locking eyes with the snake. Benito took a step back.

The blade flashed in the sun as Linford's arm swiped at the snake's head. The rattler sprang at Linford's foot, but Linford's leather boot crushed its head and pressed it deep down into the gravel. He cut its head off with another quick slice.

"Always strike first." Linford tossed the snake's limp body into the bushes beside the trail.

"Jeremiah said no weapons," said Benito, shaken by Linford's ease and speed with the knife.

"That old pappy's crazy if he thinks I ain't bringing a knife up here." Linford slid the blade back into its sheath and screwed off the top of his canteen. "Whiskey?" Benito shook his head.

"Let's get this done and then out of this godforsaken sun," Linford said, motioning for Benito to lead the way.

They pulled the mules along a steep trail, curling around the hills and winding through the broken pine trees and wilted aspens. Benito squinted up at the twin boulders forming a natural arch above them on the trail. He motioned for Linford to pause.

"This it?" called out Linford.

Before Benito could respond, a gunshot cracked the air, its echo cascading down the ridge. Linford swung his guitar case off his back and dove into the brush next to the trail. Benito waved both hands, his straw hat flapping back and forth like a peace flag.

From behind one of the leaning boulders, a lanky kid stepped forward. A smattering of whiskers covered his pink cheeks and thin neck, and a tan, wide brimmed hat concealed his eyes. Benito thought he looked no older than seventeen. He heard the boy's leather boots crunching in the gravel as he strode out onto the trail, his six-shooter aimed down at the two men.

"We don't get many folks up this way. Where you headed?"

Benito noticed him shifting his weight from one foot to the other to keep his trembling arm steady.

"We've got Everett's supplies. We don't want trouble," Benito said, fumbling in his pocket for the signed directions.

"Where's Jeremiah?" said the boy.

"Leg's still messed up," said Linford, stepping out of the brush with his guitar case in hand.

"It's why he sent me," said Benito, cutting Linford off.

"Well, if Jeremiah trusted you all, then that's good enough for me. Name's Riley. Bring the mules on up here." He paused. "After the old rebel there drops that knife, that is."

Linford's hand hovered over the knife at his belt. He stared at Riley like a slow-moving storm front, before finally setting the blade on a red rock next to the trail.

Benito went up first, and Riley led the first mule through the shaded archway into the trail on the other side. He motioned for Linford to move up next. As Benito stepped aside, he noticed Linford untying his guitar case, saw a flash of metal, and before he could react, Linford had an Army Colt pushed against Riley's back.

"Give me your pistol, and then we're going to help you bring these supplies to your camp."

Linford tossed Riley's revolver into the ravine. "Benito, grab a mule. The kid's leading now."

Benito backed away and considered making a run for it, but Linford's wild eyes were like fangs stuck in its prey. He knew if he tried to run, he'd get a bullet in his back. And Jeremiah assumed Benito would be at the rendezvous point by himself. Linford could take whatever he wanted and skip town, but Benito would be hunted for the crime.

Lucia and Rosita will be left alone. I'm trapped.

Riley's sunburned hands were raised high with Linford's gun stuck to his back like a hungry mosquito. Benito plucked off his straw hat and wiped his forehead with the back of his arm.

"This isn't good. Just let the kid go," Benito said.

"We got something bigger now—no more stealing pennies from drunks and snakes like Carlos," said Linford.

In a daze, Benito stepped back and bumped into the red rock. His fingers brushed Linford's steel blade, and he slipped the knife into his belt.

"Get up here, partner," said Linford over his shoulder.

Benito crossed himself and moved up the trail, motioning for Riley to lead the way. He would have to wait for a time to strike.

The three hiked through thicker grass and scattered evergreens, Benito clutching his rosary beads, mouthing the prayers. Except for Linford's humming, the only sounds were some hawks' screams in the distance and the relentless crunch of boots and hooves on gravel.

They finally reached the campsite, tucked inside a pocket of towering pine trees. "Where's Everett? He the only one here?" asked Linford, keeping close behind Riley as they approached.

A low flame and red embers simmered in a firepit, the smell of sapwood and scorched fish mixing with the pine needles. A couple of faded green tents pitched between the trees, and several makeshift tables contained scattered tools, rusted pickaxes, shovels, and empty mason jars.

"He was washing clothes by the river this morning. It's just us," said Riley.

"Where's the panning operation set up, kid?"

"Listen, I have a wife and kid back in town. Just take what you want and leave us be," said Riley.

"Let him go now—you don't want to do this," said Benito. Riley caught his eyes and glanced down at Benito's belt and the knife. Benito forgot he'd picked it up.

"*Amigo,* grab something to tie him to that tree," said Linford.

Riley stumbled into one of the equipment tables, his hands bracing the edge. "I need some water," he said. He caught Benito's eyes again.

"Forget the water," said Linford, prodding at Riley to stand up.

"His eyes are bugged, and he's swollen red as a pepper," said Benito. He moved in closer to Riley, handing him his canteen. Linford lowered the gun and pulled at Riley's shoulder to examine his face.

Riley took the opening and plucked the knife from Benito's belt. Riley spun on Linford and slashed at his gun hand, slicing his forearm. The Colt dropped into the dirt as Linford tripped backwards, grasping at the crimson line raging on his skin. Riley took another swipe and kicked Linford across the face then sprinted past the tents and up into the afternoon shadows of the trees.

"Son of a bitch, go after him!" said Linford, clutching his arm and scanning the ground for his revolver.

Benito's fingers curled his moustache then made the sign of the cross. He dug in his pocket for his handkerchief, and his hand touched the wooden St. Mary case he'd put there the night before. He'd forgotten it was there, but as Lucia liked to say, 'Providence had a long memory.'

Linford tied a rag around his bleeding arm. "Stop staring at me like that. We gotta clear out before Everett gets back here. Take what you can grab." Linford picked up his Colt and jogged to the nearest tent.

Benito popped the bronze latch of the St. Mary box and took out the derringer. It was the size of his left palm, and he pulled back the hammer with right thumb.

"Why are you still standing there?" said Linford, his back turned to Benito as he carried two leather pouches out of the tent. "Grab some of these pokes and let's get the hell out of here."

"We aren't going anywhere," said Benito, pointing the derringer at Linford.

Linford spun in a bluster. He saw the gun and cackled like a hyena. "That thing's smaller than your prayer beads. Put it away and help me."

"We're staying. I came to deliver Everett's supplies."

"You think he'll just shake your hand? We're both cooked when he gets here." Linford fumbled with a rope tying the poke on the mule's saddle.

The derringer shook in Benito's hand, as he aimed at Linford's leg. He'd never actually fired a gun before. It was a gift from his uncle given the night Benito and his wife left Santa Fe.

"Protect your family. Those prospectors have a bad disease in their souls. The Blessed Mother will watch over you," said his Uncle Jorge, handing him the gun in the painted case.

"Damn it, last chance or I'm leaving you here," shouted Linford, pulling tight the knot.

Benito crossed himself and fired. The bullet whizzed wide of Linford's leg, lodging itself into the thick pine bark next to him. The mule reared and a sack of flour slipped off and hit Linford's foot. Linford swung around with his Colt aimed at Benito's chest.

The men stared at each other while some agitated crows flapped and cawed in the branches. The jack-o'-lantern smile glowed on Linford's face.

"You struck first, *amigo,*" Linford said. "Problem is, you missed." He raised the revolver. "Now, it's my turn."

Benito closed his eyes, and again pulled back the hammer on the derringer. In the next heartbeat, an explosive bang ruptured the air, and Benito felt a projectile whip by him. It tore into Linford's chest and sent him flying backwards. Linford's body slammed into the pine tree then slumped down lifeless into the twisting roots at the base.

"Drop your gun," said a voice behind Benito. A man stepped out of the brush with a smoking Winchester rifle. His face was blotted with shaving cream. The only thing covering his damp, hairy chest were the suspenders holding up his canvas trousers. Benito felt the pistol in his back before he heard Riley speak behind him.

"Everett said drop it. You don't want to end up like your partner over there."

"He's not my partner." Benito handed Riley the derringer.

Everett checked Linford's pulse and shook his head. He turned to Benito. "He would've shot your head clean off before you even nicked him with that baby cap gun."

"If you hadn't given me that knife, we'd probably both be laying there right now," said Riley.

Benito handed Everett the crumpled instructions. "Linford ambushed both of us. I'm just delivering your goods."

Everett examined the paper, wiping the cream from his face. "We're going down to report this to the sheriff. You have family here?"

"Wife and daughter."

Everett motioned to Linford. "Him?"

"Maybe a cousin in Raleigh, but I doubt it. No one else I know of."

"Shame. This town only attracts the vipers now."

"Or breeds them," said Riley.

Everett went into a tent and came out with a poke. "This is for my nephew Riley's life—" he tossed Benito the pouch of gold dust.

"Do yourself a favor and get out of this place." Benito crossed himself and thought of the cool water of the acequias surrounding him as he floated between the reeds.

The next Saturday night, Rudy Carlos pushed his way through the packed saloon and noticed there wasn't any music underscoring the drunk bedlam of his establishment. He marched over to the piano, but instead of the little man sitting at the bench he found a letter. Jeremiah limped over and shouted over the noise.

"He left that for you. Asked me to write it for him. He gave me quite a going away present too." Jeremiah held up a tip jar filled with coins, with a note scribbled inside: *Todas las deudas están pagadas. Tu amigo*, Benito.

"Guess we're going to need some new players," said Jeremiah.

Carlos grabbed the letter on the bench, cigar smoke pumping out of his plump lips as he read.

"Dear Mister Carlos. Thank you for the opportunity, but this is my last odd job in Cripple Creek. I officially resign. Sincerely, Benito."

—Michael Mitchell Jr. is an author, artist, and musician living in beautiful Richmond, Virginia. Michael has a passion for storytelling and has been creating imaginative worlds and developing characters for most of his life. His work includes several children's books, as well as illustrations for comic strips and games. His short stories have appeared in Kyanite Press, Enchanted Conversation Magazine, *and* Swords & Sorcery Magazine. *Michael has taught middle school, high school, and college, and has been part of several bands. He also has directed and acted in numerous plays, including portraying Sir Thomas More in* A Man for All Seasons *and directing* The Mousetrap. *In his spare time, Michael also enjoys reading classics, playing mandolin, and watching movies. You can visit him at www.michaelmitchelljr.com.*

PURGATORY TRAIL

ROSE B. ALLEN

MILLIE MAE HAWKIN'S heart sank, as if it had slipped from her chest onto the hard soil below. The distance between where she wanted to be and where she was, well, it was farther than she could ever have imagined. Certainly, this was not part of her plan. James Fletcher's fate would just have to wait.

She ignored the scrub bristles cutting into her knees, poking through both petticoat and dress. Her satchel lay upended nearby, its scattered contents baking in the desert sun. The Celerity's tug rested unharnessed on the ground. Trail dust from the drive team's hooves lingered toward the horizon. Wasteland stretched outward into an endless expanse, dotted with sprouts of harsh green brush.

Opposite of where Millie knelt, and visible through weathered yellow wheel spokes of the coach, lay the body of the Overland Mail Company's shotgun messenger, the unlucky recipient of a single bullet to the head.

The reinsman caught one too—his to the gut. She arched over the driver, applying pressure to his abdomen with a torn rag.

Hopelessness swept through her as warm and fluid as the blood flowing over her fingers. The injured man lay several feet away from the coach against one of many stones and boulders along the trail. Next to them packed into the dirt was a solitary bloom crushed flat—its white petals splayed like a fan, its tips creating a fractured circle on the hard earth. A displaced bauble of nature.

Spent. Broken.

He loves me. He loves me not.

What did love have to do with where she was now? Love had placed her firmly in this situation. Hate would drive her through it.

The reinsman groaned. Millie shook her thoughts aside.

She leaned in closer to him, careful to be gentle. "Please remain as still as possible." Millie hollered over her shoulder to a man who cowered inside the coach.

"Mister Stanek. Please find me something to stop this bleeding."

A derby peeked from behind the window canvas, followed by a pair of round spectacles perched crookedly on the bridge of a snub nose. Its owner, Emmett Stanek, had introduced himself earlier in the journey as a man who mingled in figures, like a public accountant. "But not quite," he had added.

Stanek scoped his surroundings then pointed toward a woman sitting collapsed against a rear wheel hub. "I believe Missus Wickham keeps a handkerchief tucked in the cuff of her sleeve." Had Stanek known the older woman before boarding at Clover Ridge, he might have recognized her as a fortune teller from St. Joe and requested a future told for a coin dropped into her palm. Instead, he simply cleared his throat. "Missus Wickham, madame, if you please?"

The woman of his attention wore a traveling hat donned with puffs of black tulle and fabric flowers. The curve of its brim pushed up and away, exposing a stoic brow and a stern gaze. She was plump from years of delicacies kind to one's palette but not to one's waist. Dust coated her dress, crumpled and gathered in folds across her lap, pulled such that the hem rested above the top of her fifteen-button boots, petticoat and calves exposed. Her bosom heaved, causing white ruffles below her collar to flutter like petals bowing to a breeze. Pinned at the center of the neck band rested a brooch containing a black stone on a nest of silver filigree. The jewelry complimented her eyes—dark yet as translucent as a deathbed shroud.

Mrs. Wickham replied—however, her words were swept away by an abrupt wind gust.

Frustration clawed at Millie. "Mister Stanek, if you would *please* go through our belongings and find anything that will help stop this bleeding. Please!"

"You want me to go into the personal effects of others? Without *permission?*" His voice cracked. "What if those... devils... return while I'm elbow deep in shirts and s-shifts?"

"They got what they came for, and I guarantee they are no longer interested in our affairs."

Beneath her hands, the driver's muscles tighten.

"We must hurry, or Mister...."

"Canton," the driver said with a groan. "Charlie Canton, ma'am." He winced. Breaths came in short, quick puffs.

"Mister Canton needs our help."

Charlie sucked at air and whistled it out through coughs and broken teeth. "I'm... 'fraid too late for it, Miss."

"Never too late." A forced smile broke across her face.

The coach door creaked fully open. Stanek stretched a tentative foot outward, the heel of his shoe clicking as it settled on the step. He peered around the wagon as best he could without moving far from it. "I agree with the driver's assessment. It's too late for him."

Millie pressed harder. She wasn't going to let Canton die. She didn't know him, but she did not believe his life was worth forfeiting.

"M-miss." The cowardly bookkeeper stuttered. "This is a time to be sensible and b-brave."

She glared at him. "This man was shot because of you. If you'd given those thieves what they'd demanded the first time, we'd not be in this mess." She wiped one bloodied hand across her forehead. The chill of death kissed her brow.

Millie tilted her head toward the hot sun, closed her eyes and allowed a remembrance, gray and unclear, to cool it. *A gentle kiss.* It was a good memory that hitched itself to something evil. Primitive. Raw. A second wild gust ripped the memory from her inner brow, same as the first gust chased words from Mrs. Wickham moments ago. An involuntary yelp escaped her.

"Be thankful, Miss Hawkins," Stanek said. "If I'd waited any longer, things might have gotten worse."

Her head snapped toward him.

"Worse? Worse? How in the Good Lord's name can..."—she swatted at the scene around them— "...can this be worse?"

The rag against the driver's wound was soaked through. Millie released her hand, ripped a fresh swath of fabric from her petticoat and stacked it on top of the bloodied cloth. Canton groaned when pressure was reapplied.

Before planning her trip, she had struggled between choosing to accept what the Lord brought her or to bring justice to the man who made her life miserable. When she chose, all the plans fell into place, seaming together without effort. If only she had seen this coming. Her chin fell to her chest. The sigh that followed was heavy with bitterness and desperation. "What hope is there for us in this barren place?"

Mrs. Wickham was at her back, with an unexpectedness that forced Millie's heart to skip, and placed a hand on her shoulder. Millie twisted to see the woman.

"Miss Hawkins?" Her eyes widened and she kept her voice low. "There was a time when you thought all hope was lost. Yes? What was it? A gift? Perhaps a token?"

The question chilled her as it recalled the ethereal kiss forward. She shuddered. "It was a gesture. Long ago."

"From whom?"

Millie swallowed hard. "A friend."

"A beau?"

"Yes. My—" His name caught in her throat. "We used to meet in an attic." Heat raised to her cheeks, and they colored. The words that followed cracked. "Oh dear. Not to do anything... we were never there alone." She tugged at her ear. "Others were always with us."

"We'd thought of nothing other than what you meant, isn't that correct, Mister Stanek?" Mrs. Wickham knelt, slipping her hand under Millie's and pressed on the soddened rags. "What was the gesture?"

"A bouquet of wildflowers picked from a nearby pasture." She kept the kiss to herself.

"How did it give you hope?"

Uncertain why this woman would ask her such questions, she waited to respond and bit her lip instead. Why not? Doing so would lighten the burden of it. Why not share what ached her heart?

"Before he left to fight...." Her fingers scratched at the collar that had ripped when she had been yanked from the coach during the robbery. She stroked the tender tissue of her neck, staining it with blood. "He left a bouquet for me in the attic." The desire to return to that place grew, a great pressure pushing from the inside out. The wish for such freedom and love again was nearly unbearable.

"And where is your man now, Miss Hawkins?" Stanek moved from the coach closer to the young woman.

"Far away." She knew where he was. She couldn't say it. Millie brought her hands up to inspect. The blood, a shock of claret red and quite sticky, coated them. She scrubbed her palms on her dress. "Last I heard, he was headed to Wilson's Creek... if only...." Her words trailed off. "That was so long ago."

"If only what?" The weedy bookkeeper stepped closer.

"If only it were possible to go back." She waved over and toward the helpless tableau they all created. "Back to before all this began."

"Back to the attic?"

A flame swelled in her heart searing away any lasting drops of remaining hope. No. Never again. In that moment, Millie made another choice, one that put her back on her path. From now on, the attic, the kiss, the memories, are merely fuel for the mission.

She stood—feet firm beneath her. The trail was a hundred yards to their south. They hadn't veered too far from it. Millie had to take care of what she'd meant to do, what began her journey.

In the sky, the sun sank below its peak. The wind whipped hair across her face, dusted her with dirt, and stung at her eyes. Still, Millie saw clearly enough. She focused on the route ahead.

"How long to the nearest town?"

The reinsman said in a whisper between coughs, "You're not going into Falls Creek for some one-sided negotiatin', is ya?"

"Why do you suppose I am, Mister Canton?"

"I've seen that look before, Miss. Many times. For all your kindness, you are rank with hatred. Can smell it on ya." He tried to reposition himself against the boulder. "Rarely works in a lady's favor." More coughs rattled his chest bringing sanguine spittle to his lower lip.

She tore another swatch from her petticoat and wiped his face. "You best rest, sir."

When he was able to take a full breath, he patted his vest pocket and withdrew a flask. Millie unscrewed the cap for him. He took a long drink and relaxed. "That, and I noticed a little bottle fall from your bag."

In the clutter of her discarded satchel was a smashed bottle, its label still intact.

"Skull and bones," the driver said. "Who's the unlucky bastard?"

She pinched her eyes closed trying to bring her Elias to mind, but thoughts of him were charred with rage and revenge.

"James Fletcher." The name burned her tongue.

"Rip Fletcher?" Stanek adjusted his glasses and peered over the rims.

Her nostrils flared. "I've been told that's what folks call him."

"That's one nasty snake to be chasing after. If you don't mind me asking, what did he do to make him a marked man?"

"He'd convinced my Elias to help in getting some property back. Come to find that it wasn't his property after all. He sold it and made off with the money. The law came after my beau and caught up with him while we were together." She used the back of her wrist to try and wipe away the growing redness warming her cheeks. "Elias escaped and found the nearest regiment to enlist. I wasn't so lucky. Word got out about the two of us together. The whispers. The stares. Got so my own mother wouldn't tolerate being in my company."

"So, you're meaning to bring the war to Fletcher." Canton hacked, sending more blood onto his chin. "If you succeed, you'll live with that for an eternity. No escaping. Forgiveness is an easier path to take, Miss Hawkins." He took a messy draw from the flask.

Millie Mae helped steady his hand. "Life's hard for a woman without friends or family."

"If you succeed, ain't no taking it back. It'll be yours to live with forever. Forever is a long time. 'Specially for the lonely."

Mrs. Wickham clutched at Millie's hem. "You're going then? Into town. Alone? What if he's not there when you arrive? What if you don't arrive at all? Miss Hawkins?"

A fearful cry grew deep within Millie, and she silenced it.

The older woman let Millie's dress slip from her fingers. She rose to face the younger woman. "Very well. Clearly, you have a determined mind." She unpinned the brooch from her collar and attached it to the younger's dress, a few inches below the left shoulder.

"Take this as an object of well wishes for your protection. The trail ahead holds dangers beyond imagination. Trust yourself before others. Always be alert—and never forget...." She held Millie's gaze. "Satan lies."

Stanek piped in. "Falls Creek is about three miles beyond the bend at the Judgement Tree. Stay on the trail. It'll lead you straight into town."

Canton winked and clicked his tongue, a sign Millie took to mean, "Giddy up then, girl."

She rushed to the corpse on the opposite side of the coach and searched for his weapon. The rifle he had held had been broken apart, the result of it being struck on the iron rim of a wheel. She bent down and ran a hand along the underside of the body and grasped the pistol beneath his thigh. She lifted it, expecting it to fit awkwardly in her palm. Rocking it gently, she allowed the wood and metal to touch every part of her grip and measured its balance shift with each twist of her wrist. She grinned. It had the weight of retribution.

"Have you ever shot one of those before?" Stanek called out.

"I shot a long neck once or twice. Is it the same?"

The bookkeeper offered a terse giggle. Millie turned to the driver.

"Is shooting this pistol the same as shooting a long neck?"

"Miss. The important thing t' know is where to point and when t' shoot." The driver's chest lifted and fell. Speaking seemed such an effort. He was weak and his voice wavered. "Take the gun belt. That Colt will only get heavier the closer you get."

Millie set the shooter on the hardened soil. She rolled the body over until it was clear of the belt. The cincture was larger than expected, a wide, plain leather strip blackened from years of sweat with a few loops still holding bullets. It took a few tries to tighten it, but the last buckle hole in the leather was enough to have it rest on her hips fair enough. A single holster hung from the waist strap. She lifted the gun and pushed it into the holster. As she passed the dead man's hat, she picked it up and placed it on her head. Her gaze sharpened. She stood taller than she'd ever done before.

"Before I do what needs to get done, I'll send help."

Millie studied each person. What a ragtag quartet of survivors they were, stranded with a horseless mud wagon, broken and useless. "Mister Canton, we'll get you into the shade of the coach—"

The driver's eyelids barely covered the dead beneath them. She leaned down and caressed the lids shut. His mouth hung breathless and open, and with each attempt to close his jaw, it slackened, so she let it hang.

She grabbed the flask from his limp hand, took a swig, swished the dirt from her mouth, and then took a draw long enough to wash away the angst. She tucked the bottle between her breast and bodice, the pewter cooling her skin on contact. Millie turned toward the trail.

The harsh landscape opened before her. A dust storm thickened in the distance behind her. The town seemed a world away with no rescue in sight, and the comfort of the attic further away still. If she didn't leave now, her chances at revenge would slip away. She was ready to feed the hatred what it craved.

Had it not been clear to her before, or the other two who watched her leave, forgiveness wasn't an option for Millie Mae Hawkins.

Not now. Not ever.

—*Rose B. Allen is a short story author with published works in a variety of anthologies. Her love of Western and frontier literature began at an early age when her father encouraged her to read such classics as Harold Bell Wright's* The Shepherd of the Hills, *and just about any story written by Louis L'Amour. Since then, she has embraced the history and lore of the American West. Rose earned a Bachelor of Arts degree in English from the University of Missouri, St. Louis. She's been an active member of the Missouri writing group, Saturday Writers, since 2014, working to support other writers in achieving their best work. She held many positions with the non-profit including membership coordinator, secretary, and director. She was fortunate to have had many addresses in the United States and Europe over the years. When it came time to stake her claim, she returned to the place she loved best, just west of the Mississippi where she lives*

On the Skirmish Line by Charles Schreyvogel

KACHINA'S DANCE

GINGER STRIVELLI

KACHINA PULLED HERSELF up from her sleeping mat. She listened to her joints pop and crack with a sigh and a laugh. She wasn't young anymore, not that she had ever been as graceful and agile as her name suggested. She was no 'spirit dancer.' She had never been able to dance with her disability. She was able to do other magical work nonetheless. She was her Hopi tribe's most honored magic worker.

She retrieved her cane from the corner of her pueblo. She didn't loathe it like the other elders loathed theirs. She didn't see it as proof of being elderly. She had used it since she was seven summers old and finally learned to walk on her own. After those seven years of being unable to run along and play with the other children, that cane was a sign of success, not a sign of age to Kachina. One could tell it was a beloved treasure by looking at it. It was beautifully carved with magical signs and painted with totem animal spirits. When Kachina took it in her hand, the opal stone at the top glowed from within with a magical powered ancient spell. The spell that made it light up also gave Kachina the needed extra strength to make her legs hold her weight in spite of their deformity.

This was the way that all of Kachina's days started, but this wasn't just another day. This was the first of her final days on Mother Earth. Today she would start to look for the tribe's new magic worker to replace her. Her spirit guides had come to her in her dreams that night and told her it was time for her to leave this life. She needed to prepare herself and the village for her absence because her days were numbered, numbered to exactly twenty-eight.

She had just one moon cycle to prepare herself and her village. She had no doubt she would be ready. She was eighty-seven. She had been ready to go for quite some time. The village, however, needed someone to call the prey animals to the hunters, to deliver the babies, to banish the curses and fevers, to pronounce the marriage rites, and to call the spirits to the dead's funeral plots. Kachina had to find them a new magic worker.

"Where to start?" She asked the Tawa, the Sun God, as she exited her pueblo. He didn't answer her in words anyone else could hear, nonetheless, Kachina nodded to the answer she heard Him offer.

She limped off toward the center of her village. She knew she'd not find a new magic worker there. She had lived in that village all the days of her life, and alas, both of her apprentices had died before her. She meant to ask the Chief if she could travel out to the surrounding villages to speak to their medicine men and women. None of them were truly magic workers but perhaps one could progress to that station and take over Kachina's job for her village, she thought.

"Kachina, your own spirit guides told you that you were dying, do you really think you should be traveling around the plains?" The Chief shook his head. "I shall send word to the other Chiefs that they should send their medicine people here to meet with you."

"Very well. That is likely wiser." Kachina agreed. "I shall go prepare my pueblo for my guests."

Kachina's pueblo was big enough for many guests. Though she had never married, never bore children, the tribe had built her one of the largest homes. Of course, she often used it as a sick room in her role as healer, so it was more of a public building than a private home.

The next day at noon her first guest arrived. Crying Owl was a young woman from the village to the East. Kachina had heard she was an accomplished healer and midwife but a rather unremarkable magician.

Within minutes, the second arrived. A medicine man named Red Rock Bridge was well known to be capable both at healing and magic, but of course he was not a midwife, and he was nearly as old as Kachina herself, worrisomely.

Later, from the Northern Village came Little Quiet One. She was neither of those things. She was a great big strong woman, swollen even more than usual with the impending birth of her fifteenth child, who spoke constantly of the other fourteen. Kachina knew that Little Quiet One worked mighty spells, made wonderful charms, but despite her own fertility, struggled with the healing and midwifery arts.

Lastly arriving was Tornado. He was said to be the greatest healer and magician the village to the south had ever known. In fact, Kachina knew many people whispered that he claimed he was better than Kachina herself. Along with Tornado came a maid servant, whom he called Shadow. Though, Kachina had delivered the child and clearly recalled her mother naming her Fire Spirit.

With all the local magicians present, Kachina began the interviews. First she asked them to cast some simple spells. She directed them to make her cold fire pit light itself and then extinguish itself. They all managed those two spells, though Crying Owl struggled. Tornado had rudely commented that she needed to practice more. Little Quiet One had assured her to keep trying.

Finally, on her third attempt she managed to get the fire to spark alive. Then it took her only one failed attempt before being able to make it magically wink out again.

Kachina next asked each to prescribe something magical, not herbal to help her pain. Tornado made her a medicine bag to wear around her neck filled with black silvery stones that he had Fire Spirit bring him from a large basket of supplies they had brought. It would be some comfort, if worn, Kachina knew. Crying Owl gave her a tiny metal-filled gourd bell. She told Kachina to shake it in her left hand when in pain and that would indeed provide some relief. Red Rock

Bridge gave her a spoken incantation to chant to lessen her aches that he said he used to quiet his own aches. Little Quiet One simply laid her hands upon both of Kachina's knees, instantly lifting most of the pain out of them, though the effects faded quickly once Little Quiet One took her hands away.

Finally, Kachina took them out of the central village on foot to gather healing herbs. Tornado's maid servant stayed behind and said she would prepare their evening meal. The herbal hunt wasn't helpful to Kachina because she found all her guests were equally capable at finding, identifying, and correctly gathering the medicinal herbs. Once back at her lodge, she directed them to prepare the herbs for storage, but again found each one was able to crush, oil, press, dry, and pack each herb just exactly as it should be.

"Is our meal ready, Shadow?" Tornado asked as he set the final basket of herbs on Kachina's shelves.

"Nearly, Magician Tornado." She answered formally. "I will fetch it from the fire."

"I will help Fire Spirit with our food. The four of you can go wash up in the river," Kachina said. Once the others had left she said to the girl, "Fire Spirit, why does Tornado call you Shadow?"

"The Magician always says Fire Spirit does not suit me." She was carrying a wooden platter with several fried fish, and she let Kachina carry the basket full of corn cakes. "Then, in one of his visions, the Great Spirit told him I was like his shadow, so he began calling me that."

"Are you Tornado's wife as well as his apprentice?" Kachina sat down, with her usual pops and cracks coming from her twisted legs, by the mat where Fire Spirit was laying out their meal.

"Not yet, either wife or apprentice... just his servant, but I hope to be both one day."

As the others returned, Kachina asked Crying Owl to say a thanksgiving prayer over their food. Kachina took Little Quiet One's hand to her right, and Fire Spirit's to her left. The others all joined hands and looked skyward out of the pueblo's smoke hole.

Crying Owl cleared her throat. "Father Sky, Mother Earth, Sister

Moon, and our Star Brothers, we offer you our usual thanks for this food, this life, this day. Bless us with many more."

Everyone began to fill their bowls and eat. Kachina looked over the group as she nibbled on a corn cake. She thought Crying Owl was the most logical replacement for herself even if the woman was only slightly above average magically. Little Quiet One was capable and entertaining but too grounded in her children's lives to devote herself fully as the tribe's magic worker. Red Rock Bridge was so old he'd need a replacement of his own too soon, and Tornado was unsuitable despite his village's high opinion of him, Fire Spirit's higher opinion of him, and his highest opinion of himself. Kachina decided to conduct one more test before confirming her choice.

After dinner, Kachina motioned for the others to join her around the pueblo's fire pit. "My mother named me Kachina, because upon seeing my twisted legs, she thought that I would not live and she sought to ensure in the afterlife that I would not be crippled and be able to walk, run, and dance with the other spirits. Alas, I lived, even walked, tried to run, but alas, I never danced. I have been told by my spirit guides that I shall die soon and finally dance in spirit form as my mother had wished for me to be able to do. Nonetheless, I long to dance here on Mother Earth, in this life, before I go to the spirit world. How would each of you help me to experience a real dance here before I pass into the next life?"

Red Rock Bridge spoke first. "I would put you in a trance and convince you that you had indeed danced. You would recall it perfectly when I awoke you."

Tornado grunted. "I would have you truly experience the dance, not just falsely remember it."

"How?" Kachina asked intrigued.

"There is an herb that if eaten or smoked, you would dance, and you'd never know you were not dancing perfectly well," Tornado said.

"Ah, but she would not remember dancing then." Red Rock Bridge shook his head. "What is the point of dancing, if she does not remember doing so?"

"I'd not truly be dancing, either. I'd be hobbling around like a crippled old woman too out of my senses to know better," Kachina said disappointedly.

"You should have had children. I enjoy my children's accomplishments as if they were my own," Little Quiet One said. "You should have had a daughter and had her trained as a dancer."

"I have no answer to your riddle, Manitou," Crying Owl said. "I can think of no magic or medicine that would make you really dance."

"Perhaps," Fire Spirit said timidly. "You could use my body."

"Hush, Shadow!" Tornado barked at his maid servant with a dismissive wave.

"No. Go on, Fire Spirit. How is such a thing possible?" Kachina asked. She had not expected to hear the correct answer from anyone, much less the maid servant.

"I can leave my body...." Fire Spirit began.

Kachina interrupted her. "You have done so before?"

"Yes, I learned it as a child. It's not difficult for me. Then after I leave, you can leave your own body. You can, can't you?" She waited for Kachina to nod before continuing. "You shall enter my body and I shall enter yours. We can't stay switched for too long, I imagine, but probably long enough for you to dance. Then we just follow our silver cords back into our own bodies afterward."

"She does not have the knowledge or the power to conduct such a magical feat. I however, do. You can use *my* body," Tornado said.

"No. I shall use Fire Spirit's body. If she is willing?"

"Of course, Kachina. It will take me a moment." Fire Spirit closed her eyes and did nothing else that could be seen by the others.

After a few breaths, Kachina recognized that Fire Spirit had vacated her body. Kachina lowered her head, closed her eyes, and faster than the younger woman, but in the same manner, by the same magic, lifted out of her body.

Suddenly, the others all saw Fire Spirit leap to her feet. She danced the graceful Butterfly dance all about the lodge. Then she danced the Hoop Dance, somehow not even needing the hoops as she circled the fire three times. Lastly, she improvised a slow sorrowful dance back to her seat and sunk back to the cold hard ground.

After both women's spirits returned to their own bodies, Fire Spirit's eyes flew open. "Oh, Kachina, I wish I could have seen you dance. I could not get your eyes to open for me."

"I will teach you to control the host body, before I die. Fire Spirit, you are to be the tribe's new magic worker."

"You must be senile, Kachina!" Tornado jumped to his feet. "She isn't a good choice at all. She is just an idiot child. I don't even know why I suffer through having her follow me around like an orphaned wolf pup."

"You suffer it because, though you have the knowledge to work your spells, you must draw the power from someone who is more gifted in magic than you. Fire Spirit has yet to learn she has that power, and yet to learn you were just using her and did not intend to ever make her your apprentice or your bride," Kachina said with a shake of her head making her gray braids bounce on her shoulders.

"She's not worthy of being my apprentice, or my bride, or your replacement." Tornado got up and stormed out of the lodge rather like his namesake twister.

Kachina ignored the outburst and turned to Fire Spirit. "You will be worthy to be the new magic worker, and you are worthy to be my apprentice now, albeit briefly. I will teach you all you need to know to be the magic worker in my dying days this moon cycle. Also, you are worthy to be a much better man's bride someday as well, my dear." Kachina held her hand out to Fire Spirit. "Will you accept your fate to become the tribe's magic worker upon my death?"

Fire Spirit had watched the door flaps flutter in Tornado's wake, until they fell still. She looked back at Kachina as a single tear dropped from her left eye. "I shall be honored to learn from you, Kachina."

The others congratulated Fire Spirit on being chosen and congratulated Kachina on finding her replacement before they all departed for their home villages.

Just as her guides had promised her, Kachina did die peacefully in her sleep twenty-eight days afterwards. In the afterlife, Kachina danced!

———————————✦———————————

—Ginger Strivelli is a disabled artist and writer from North Carolina, USA. She has written for Marion Zimmer Bradley's Fantasy Magazine, Circle Magazine, Third Flatiron, Autism Parenting Magazine, Silver Blade, Solarpunk Magazine, The New Accelerator, *various other magazines and several anthology books. She loves to travel the world and make arts and crafts. She considers herself a storyteller entertaining and educating through her writing.*

OFF DUTY COP

ELIZABETH FACKLER

AS THEY SAT in Debra's car after dinner, Teresa wore a white eyelet blouse and a short skirt, her dusky skin as smooth as whipped chocolate.

Debra was in her usual outfit of jeans, a sleeveless tee, and her light linen jacket to hide the holstered gun in the back of her belt. It was licensed in Texas, but she was in Tucson parked in front of the house Teresa shared with her mother and brother.

Debra had been staying over the last few weeks and had known this conversation was apt to come up. She looked out at the neighborhood of adobe homes with rock-strewn cactus gardens.

"Weren't you, like, you know, curious?" Teresa asked.

"No."

Teresa's smile quivered as she glanced at Debra from beneath mascara-laden lashes. "I went through years at the beginning when I couldn't get enough. Wasn't 'til I was twenty-two that I figured out it wasn't there."

Debra watched her nestled against the door, voluptuous and vulnerable with the street savvy of a kid who grew up tough and became a cocktail waitress, cashing in on pretending to be helpless.

Teresa tapped her nails nervously on a bare knee. "How old were you when you first slept with a woman?"

"Seventeen. An older friend seduced me."

"Was it good? I mean, did you like it?"

"It was both bizarre and beautiful."

Teresa nodded. "So when was the first time you did it, you know, for real?"

"Two years ago."

"You're kidding!"

Debra shook her head.

"You didn't do nothing 'tween when you were seventeen and two years ago?"

"I played around some, but I wasn't in love."

"So what happened?"

"My job got intense, and I was putting her in danger, so I left 'em both behind."

The bronze gloss on Teresa's lips glistened in the dim light from the porch. "That's why you're in Tucson."

Debra nodded, watching Teresa's brother park his Chevy low-rider in the driveway and stalk into the house.

Teresa sighed. "He looks pissed off."

"Isn't he always?"

She sighed again, a long slow slide.

Not for the first time, Debra suggested, "Why don't we get our own place?"

"I can't leave my mother alone with him."

Debra was thinking she might as well deal with the demons she had left in Fort Worth as waste energy on Teresa's brother, a vato riding anger and disappointment to destruction.

Teresa's smile was teasing. "He knows about us."

"Did you think he wouldn't?"

She shrugged, then giggled. "You'll stay tonight?"

Debra leaned across and kissed her, getting lost for a moment in her jasmine perfume.

"Yeah, I can stay the night."

Celia looked up from the TV as they came in. A short, round woman with saggy jowls, bright red lipstick, and exaggerated arched eyebrows. She had her glossy black curls dyed and styled in a beauty parlor every week. Debra thought she looked like a melancholy clown. Her usual rap a litany of complaints. Tonight she greeted them with, "You're late."

"We went driving, Ma." Teresa leaned to kiss her cheek.

Debra sank into the rocker, watching them. The living room was kept immaculate by Celia, who worked around the house each morning and spent the rest of her days under a green-and-yellow afghan watching Mexican soap operas on TV. The sofa was a plush chocolate brown, the purple paisley rocker the only other seat. The wall opposite it held three framed prints—Jesus Christ, the Virgin of Guadalupe, and JFK. In front of the sofa, the television was flanked by built-in shelves lined with photographs of Teresa and Alejandro growing up, along with a few of their father as a young man with one or the other of them on his knee. He had been killed in a drug deal when Alejandro was two and Teresa four, but his influence ricocheted in his son's inept criminality. At twenty-five, Teresa was the mainstay of the family.

"You need anything?" she asked her mother. "Want me to make you some tea or a sandwich?"

"No, my stomach's upset. I'll just leave it alone."

"Pepcid? You want a Pepcid, Ma?"

She shook her head. "Your brother's in the kitchen. Maybe he wants something."

Teresa dropped her purse on the sofa. "I'm sure he knows how to get it." She walked into the dark hall toward the bathroom.

Debra and Celia met each other's eyes. Debra smiled.

"So you took my daughter driving," Celia said.

Debra nodded.

They looked back at the screen—a blonde in a pink peignoir pleading with a man in a dark suit. Debra had to concentrate to follow any Spanish conversation, and for this, she didn't bother. "You should come to dinner with us some time, Celia."

"Only gypsies eat in restaurants."

Debra laughed. "So pretend you're a gypsy."

Celia looked over in astonishment. "You're a funny girl. Do you think people can just change who they are?"

"Why don't you try it?"

"There are things I would like to change," she said, watching the screen. "I would like my back to not hurt so I could work again. Teresa should get married, but what man'll take on a crippled mother-in-law?"

Ducking the mention of a husband, Debra said gently, "Anyone who loves her."

The sharp black eyes pinned her sitting with the ankle of one dusty boot resting on her Levi-clad knee. "You love her?"

"Yeah, I do."

"Huh." She looked back at the screen. "You don't even have a job. You're like Alejandro—another problem, not a solution."

"Why don't you kick him out?"

Celia stared straight ahead, as if she hadn't heard.

"He's of age," Debra said. "Let him stand on his own."

The wrinkled old neck swiveled around so the black eyes, now moist with tears, met Debra's. "This is his home. He's welcome long as he wants to stay." She looked back at the screen. "So are you."

Debra smiled. "Thanks, Celia, but I'll be moving on tomorrow."

"What's Teresa think of that?"

"I asked her to come with me."

"She said no, didn't she. 'Cause of me. Isn't that what she said?"

Debra nodded.

"Why can't you stay?"

"Alejandro and I don't mix."

"So let him be. He'll find his way."

"I think he's gonna make a mess getting there."

He lumbered in from the kitchen, his black crew topping a bullet-shaped head with a face full of hate. "Nobody calls me a mess in my own house."

Debra watched him.

"Don't start," Celia said. "I'm trying to hear this program."

Alejandro spotted Teresa's purse on the sofa. He walked over and took a twenty from her wallet. Smirking, he turned back into the kitchen. Teresa came out of the bathroom and joined him there. Debra could hear their voices but not catch the Spanish words, though Teresa's tone was conciliatory, his surly.

Carrying a half-eaten burrito wrapped in a napkin, he walked through the living room and out the front door.

Teresa came in and saw her open purse. She took out her wallet and counted what was left. "That sonofabitch," she muttered, spinning toward the door. His car roared as she yelled, "Give that back, *pendejo!*" His tires screeched as he accelerated out of the driveway. "Sonofabitch!" she screamed as he peeled rubber on the street. The silence was heavy when she shut the door. "Why didn't you tell me he got into my pocketbook?"

Debra and Celia didn't answer, all three of them knowing it would only have prolonged the scene. Teresa stalked across to scoop her purse off the sofa. "I'm going to bed."

Debra watched anger stiffening Teresa's naturally fluid stride, then looked at her mother.

"One of these days," Celia said, staring at the screen, "he'll make money again and these things won't happen."

Debra followed Teresa into her room, sat down on the bed, and watched her crying on the stool in front of her vanity. It had a homemade skirt sewn by Celia of pink gingham. Teresa had been twelve then. Now she looked up, her eyes red and her mascara streaked.

"Are we having fun yet?" Debra asked.

Teresa laughed. "Same old shit, ain't it."

Debra nodded and slumped on the bed.

She slept sans panties in oversize tee-shirts. Teresa favored cotton nightgowns. Debra liked her best in bed, without makeup or the risque outfits she wore for work. Alone under the covers, they created a cocoon of camaraderie so close they were like children in their lack of modesty. To Teresa's blind groping, Debra was the guiding light. All that was lost, however, on the streets. Prowling the city while Teresa worked, Debra felt beat. According to a personality test given in the army, her psychological driver was an androgynous prick named *Be Perfect.* It had enhanced her rise through law enforcement and earned her commendations for being cool under fire, but when faced with an undeniable evil it threw up its hands in defeat. Having always been near the top of her class, driving midnight streets with the dregs of the unemployed felt like skirting a funnel to failure. Her only current challenge was Alejandro, a specimen of macho arrogance she especially despised. One night on her aimless wandering through town, she drove back to Celia's house and parked at the curb. The driveway was empty, Alejandro not home. She used her key to let herself in.

Celia looked over her shoulder and smiled. "You're back early, *mija.*"

Debra sat on the end of the sofa and watched Celia watching TV. Her double chin and flabby arms were a testament to her impairment. "What do you think's gonna happen with Alejandro?"

Celia glanced over. After a moment, she sighed, her eyes on the screen. "He'll be killed doing something foolish like his father."

Debra nodded. "Why don't you put your foot down?"

"I stand my ground, *mija.* What else can I do?"

"Stand his."

Celia glared at her. "Maybe it's easy for you who knows only strangers. You speed this way and that in your fast car so people only see a blur on the street. When you live in the same house, like me, for thirty years, people are more than what they do."

"All I'm saying, Celia, is he makes your life hell because you allow it."

"Maybe someday I won't," she said, her gaze again on the screen.

Debra washed her hands in the bathroom, then met her eyes in the mirror. "Maybe someday I won't either," she said.

SITTING AT THE bar in The Rattlesnake's Lair, watching Teresa clean up after closing, Debra didn't want to go back to the house. Bored with being loose, she felt eager to pull in harness again but wasn't on anyone's team.

Ben took her empty glass to wash in the sink. His friendship had attracted her to the club and would have kept her coming back even if Teresa wasn't there. With a savvy smile, he said, "You're off your oats."

She nodded. "It's time I hit the road."

He looked at Teresa wiping the table in the back corner booth. "She'll be done in a minute."

"That's not what I meant."

He pulled the plug in the sink. Above the gurgle of water eddying down the drain, he said, "I'm surprised you've stayed this long."

"Why?"

"Let's just say you don't vacation well." He chuckled. "You're chomping at the bit, girl, stomping in the corral ready to run. You oughta jump the fence and shake that burr out from under your tail."

Laconically, she asked, "Which burr is that?"

"Whatever drove you out of Texas."

Debra nodded. "What I should be doing is called taking your pharmaceuticals."

"Sometimes that's better than self-medicating," he said.

BEING DRIVEN HOME through the dark streets, Teresa was tired. Debra decided to wait until morning to announce she was leaving. But shortly past dawn, she woke to Alejandro yelling at his mother. Debra looked at the woman beside her, able to sleep through quarrels that wore on her nerves, then lay back and stared at the ceiling, feeling anger coil in her spine.

"I don't care," Alejandro shouted. "You're just a useless old mule."

"This is my house," Celia replied. "I'll say what I want."

Debra eased herself from bed, opened the drapes, and stood staring out at the yard, a shadowed, barren patch inside a stone wall. In the corner, a dilapidated swing-set rusted beneath the unkind sunlight. Admiring Teresa's long, dark hair tangled across the pale sheet. Debra wondered how long she might have stayed if Alejandro weren't here, if Teresa might not have become the lover she dallied with then never left. If she didn't go back to Fort Worth, her future was wide open, her career at a dead stop. Why not Teresa and Tucson?

She heard glass shatter against a wall.

Teresa woke up, yanking herself erect in fear.

Debra pulled on her jeans, heavy with the .38 in her belt. "I'll handle it." She didn't look back as she walked barefoot down the hall. Her long tee-shirt concealing her weapon.

Alejandro stood like a menacing gorilla staring at a wet stain on the wall adjacent to his mother huddled on the sofa. The stain was closer to Jesus than the Virgin Mary, ice and shards of glass in a puddle on the carpet. Celia sat cowering under her afghan, her arms crooked over her head, and the silent TV flashing bright colors.

"Quit being an ass, Alejandro," Debra said from the door.

He wheeled around. "You ain't got no right to tell me nothin'. What d'ya think of that?"

"I think it's stupid."

"You calling me stupid?"

"No, you're smart. You just don't act like it."

"You see," Celia said, picking at the fuzz on her afghan.

Alejandro sank into the rocker and glared at Debra. "She oughta be paying rent."

"She is," Celia said.

"I ain't seen none of it."

"Why should you?"

"This is my father's house, and I'm the man here now. I oughta get a cut of that money."

"If you're the man of the house," Celia demanded, "you're s'posed to give us money, not steal from your sister. Debra's more man than you are."

Debra winced.

Alejandro flashed a ribald grin. "Looks to me like she's got tits, though they ain't very big."

Conscious of her nipples poking from beneath her tee, she privately admitted his breasts were indeed bigger and a lot flabbier.

Celia twisted around to study her in the doorway. "Why don't you sit down, *mija?*"

"She's not your daughter," Alejandro said.

Debra walked past him and sat near Celia. Gently she told the old woman, "You know this never gets us anywhere."

Celia used the remote to raise the sound on the TV. "So where we going?"

Debra looked at Alejandro. His face screwed with unspent rage.

"Why is it you sleep with girls?" he asked. "Ain't you never had a man stick it to you?"

"Hush, Alejandro," Celia scolded. "You don't use such language in front of your mother."

"I'm talking to her. I want to know."

Debra held herself in check. "Doesn't mean you're gonna find out."

"Why not?"

"It's none of your business."

"You're sleeping with my sister."

"That's her decision, not yours."

"How does she know who you've been with? Maybe you'll give her a disease."

"She's more likely to catch one cleaning up after you."

He snorted disbelief.

"I'm trying to hear this program," Celia said.

They all watched a curvaceous blonde chastise a blushing young man.

"Twenty years ago that would've never happened," Alejandro said. No one answered him.

"She deserves a smack on the face."

"Your father never hit me," Celia said, looking straight at him. "Never once did he raise his hand."

"He hit *me,*" Alejandro mumbled.

"Don't tell me that. I was there. You were just a baby."

"All the men I know hit their women."

"Maybe 'cause you know the wrong kinda men." Celia kept her eyes on the screen.

"S'pose Debra here's the right kind, eh?"

"Least she don't steal for a living. You're not even a good crook."

"What d'you know?"

She met his eyes. "Good criminals have money."

Teresa came in wearing her fuzzy pink bathrobe. "What's going on? Some kinda family powwow?"

"We're deciding your brother's future," Celia said, staring at the screen.

Snuggling close with the moist smell of sleep, Teresa mumbled to Debra, "You want to be in on this?"

"I'm here," Debra said, meeting Alejandro's eyes.

"Ain't they cute?" he minced. "Lesbian lovers cozy on the couch."

Teresa sat up, holding Debra's hand. "Where's your lover, Alejandro? How come you never bring a girl home?"

"Maybe I'm ashamed of it."

"How do you say that?" Celia snapped. "We have a nice house."

For the first time, Debra saw contrition on his face.

"There's nothing wrong with it," he replied. "You keep it nice, Ma."

"With no help from you," she muttered, looking back at the screen.

"What is it you want, *hermano?*" Teresa asked earnestly. "We all love you here."

He glared at Debra. "She doesn't."

"She loves me," Teresa said. "That means she cares about you 'cause I do."

He shifted his gaze to the screen, a close-up of a couple kissing in bed. "I want life to be easy."

"It isn't," Celia said.

"Nothing I try works out!" he cried.

"Try doing something right," she said.

"Like what?" he asked.

"Get a job," Debra said.

He smirked. "So I could bring home four C's a week? I can make that in one deal."

"Why don't you?" his mother asked.

"Like I said," he mumbled. "Things ain't worked out lately."

"You're gonna end up in jail." Celia pinned her dark eyes on Debra. "Is true, eh?"

"It's likely."

"Maybe I'll beat the odds."

Debra shrugged.

"You're so damn cool, sitting there with your tits sticking out. Why don't you put on a bra?"

"Know what I'm gonna do?" She stood up. "I'm gonna go pack."

Teresa looked up, biting her lip.

Leaving the room, Debra heard Celia scold, "See what you do!"

Debra closed the door and turned on the overhead light. The bed covers were draped following Teresa's exit, and the vanity's mirror reflected Debra's image. She looked at herself in the smock-like tee over jeans, her hair uncombed and sticking up in back, thinking family combat rarely caught you at your best. She pulled her battered suitcase from under the bed.

A brown leather box that held the scant possessions she had been carting around since leaving Fort Worth—a few pieces of jewelry, a week's supply of undies, a couple pairs of jeans, half a dozen tees, a jogging suit and shoes, two tailored blouses, a skirt, and loafers for when she wanted a change. She sat on the bed and pulled on her knee-high boots bought in Tombstone. Pushing six feet when she stood up on their solid wood heels, she had become so accustomed to the boots' comfort she wondered why she had never tried them before. Belatedly, she realized that growing up in Texas she had spurned asserting the aggression of masculine shoes. Smiling at the cowardice of her youth, she shrugged into her jacket as she headed down the hall for her toothbrush.

Passing the living room, she heard Alejandro say, "You're a whoring bitch. I bet you sleep with all your customers."

Debra stepped into the room. "Don't talk to your sister like that."

"Look at you," he said, "wearing a bra."

"Did you hear what I said?"

"Yeah, and you wanna see something? Watch this." He stood up and slapped Teresa's face, making her cry out and cringe against her mother as he grinned at Debra.

"Aye," Celia whimpered.

Debra strode in and chopped his trachea with the edge of her hand.

He staggered backward, clutching his throat as he stumbled into the rocker.

"What's the matter, tough boy?" Debra mocked. "Can't catch your breath?"

A sick growl strangled from his throat.

Teresa said softly, "You can kill someone like that."

"Yeah, you can," Debra agreed. "But I know what I'm doing, 'cept for being here. I don't know what the hell I'm doing here."

Teresa smiled, her cheek still pink from her brother's palm. "You brought me home one night and stayed. Remember?"

Debra nodded, regretfully shifting her focus to Alejandro. "But I won't stay with him."

"Who's asking you to?" he said.

"I am," Teresa said, meeting Debra's eyes.

"Me, also," Celia said.

They all looked at Alejandro, his face mottled as he sat limp, and his arms at his sides.

"You should go," Celia told him sadly. "I accept it when you hit me 'cause I'm your mother, and what you are is my fault. But you can't hit your sister. That I don't allow."

"What d'you mean," he said, "what I am is your fault?"

"Who else's? Were you born a bitter man who takes his hurt out on his family?"

He struggled to his feet. "If you don't want me around, I don't need you."

"Fine!" Celia said. "I wish you well."

Throwing Debra a cowed glance, he lumbered from the room. They all listened to his closet bang open, drawers being yanked from his bureau, the heavy tread of his steps and labored pant of his breath. He came back carrying a cardboard suitcase, but stopped halfway to the front door and looked at the three of them, Debra still standing,

Teresa huddled on the sofa, and his mother fumbling for something beneath herself.

"Take it," she said, extending a roll of money held tight by a rubberband. "Is all I have, so don't come asking for more."

He had to step closer to reach it. Debra backed out of his way. He stood staring down at his mother as if unable to find the words to thank her.

"You can come home," she said, "when you have something good to give us."

He looked at Teresa, who gave him a hopeful smile, then at Debra. She kept her face neutral, already backpedaling out.

"See you around," he said, and she didn't know if it was a threat for the streets or a promise to return.

They watched him leave, then listened to him quietly start his car and drive away.

Celia turned the television off and sighed. "Now we have only us."

Teresa laughed. "And peace and quiet." She gave Debra a grateful smile.

Celia moaned, pushing herself off the sofa. "I'm going back to bed, *mijas.*" She left her afghan in a crumpled pile.

They watched her walk stiffly into the hall and listened to her bedroom door close before looking at each other.

"So now what?" Teresa asked.

"I'm going home," Debra said. "I've got to give notice at work, get my stuff out of Samantha's house, and say goodbye to a couple o' people."

"Will you come back?"

Debra shrugged. "I have to figure out who I am."

"Who you are is a woman who can hold her own. But I think what you're really saying is you're not a cop anymore."

"Can't be a cop without a badge."

"You did pretty good tonight," Teresa said.

Driving east through the empty desert, Debra decided Teresa had deliberately taken her home to render Alejandro harmless. Debra had never minded standing up for people she cared about, but now it seemed like an extension of her job, and she resented being confined to one facet of herself. She supposed her professional slip had cracked that expertise too. There was a time when she felt in control. Now she felt like a loose ball in a pinball machine.

Speeding across the barren prairie in her low, fast car, she vowed that if she managed to skate free after having killed a corrupt cop, she would find someone who could love her even if she never again owned the wisdom to sport a badge.

———◆———

—Elizabeth Fackler writes of the American Southwest, past and present. Her novel, My Eyes Have A Cold Nose, *won the best historical fiction award in the New Mexico Book Awards of 2009, and her novel,* Bone Justice, *was a finalist in 2006. Western Writers of America called her* Billy the Kid: The Legend of El Chivato *"a magnificent achievement in historical fiction." Her poem "Taos II" was included in the* New Mexico Poetry Anthology of 2023 *published by the Museum of New Mexico. The New York Times called her "a fine writer." Library Journal said, "her elegant prose is a pleasure to read." Award-winning author Ed Gorman said, "She makes familiar elements startling and new through the dazzle of her prose and the humanity of her forgiving gaze." The Kirkus Review of her latest novel,* To the Bone, *said, "She tells a good story, keeps things moving, and dishes up surprises aplenty." She lives in the mountains of southern Colorado with her musician husband and Aussie Chloe.*

EL DESEO

JOHN A. TURES

"ARE YOU SURE the ghost town is around here, Uncle Josh?" Winnie asked, peering through the scrub brush, weeds, and trees on the overgrown trail in Southern New Mexico on their morning hike.

"Yeah, we want to see where the famous gunfights took place." Josh's nephew had found a stick with a branch, the whole thing intended to resemble a pistol.

"I saw it on a Boy Scout hike growing up," history teacher Joshua Fletcher insisted to his grade-school-age nieces and nephews. That excursion brought back memories of what was supposed to be a campout within the confines of the old Western town of El Deseo. But not long after they reached the ruins, his scoutmaster, Mr. Baugh hustled them out of the town to the surprise of everyone.

He overheard the elderly leader whispering to the other adults. "That fog rolling in is bad news."

They shrugged but complied. Mr. Baugh barked at the scouts to hurry along the path, like he was back in Korea, fleeing the Chinese People's Liberation Army. Not until they drove off minutes before the mist came to the parking lot did the old scoutmaster seem to relax. They reconvened near the ruins of a pueblo more than an hour away.

"Will it still be there?" His other nephew Ben asked.

"Wood rots, you know," Winnie replied.

"It burned a few years after the residents built the town when they found silver." Josh felt like he was back at Alexandria Academy, teaching history to high schoolers. "They rebuilt it with stone and adobe...."

"I see it!" chirped Thelma, his younger niece.

Sure enough, through the Ponderosa pines and scrub brush, El Deseo emerged. Covered in vines, several of the buildings were still standing, though the General Store's roof and one side had collapsed. It was just the way he remembered it from Boy Scout days.

He called the four kids back to take a selfie with him before letting them explore the ghost town. He was Uncle Josh, the cool adult. While their parents slept in the rental cabin a mile away, he would take them on all kinds of adventures on their trips, from beaches to amusement park rides.

Once, on an early morning stroll through Washington, D.C., eight-year-old nephew Ben informed him that they needed an adult with them to cross the street. Winnie laughed. "Uncle Josh is an adult!" Ivy, his girlfriend, an art teacher at Alexandria Academy where he taught, remarked the other night when she joined them on this family trip. "The kids see you as one of them. It's a compliment!"

"Yeah," Josh had replied. "I get that."

"You might be a pretty good dad yourself, you know," Ivy added, curling her fingers around his arm.

"I don't know," he said evasively. "Kids are fun in short bursts, but they're a lot of responsibility. And they're expensive too. I doubt our combined teaching salaries could afford even one."

The art teacher pouted slightly. "I'd like to try, at least."

Josh shrugged. "Maybe in a few years, we'll have enough."

"Money or kids?" she laughed.

"Dad, I mean, Uncle Josh," Ben snapped him back to reality. The kids were always doing that. "Can we go into the saloon?"

"Hell yeah... I mean, heck yeah!" Josh replied in a fake Texas accent. Was it his swearing or voice that made the kids giggle?

"Uncle Josh, we already know most of the swear words," Thelma said.

"Thanks to Uncle Josh." Kit snickered as the other kids laughed.

"Well, you can't say I haven't educated you on something at least."

Inside the Sunset Saloon, they tickled the ivories on the player piano, inspected the dusty bottles behind the bar, and sat at the stools, ordering fake Sarsaparilla.

"Can we go upstairs, Uncle Josh?" Kit asked, already trying out the first step. The wood groaned under his ten-year-old weight.

"Uh… better pass on that, kids," Josh said. "You don't want to crash through the steps, break a leg, and have to miss the baseball season." His brother-in-law, the attorney, would probably sue him.

Kit rapidly withdrew his foot, equally nervous about such an injury.

"What would the people here do upstairs?" Thelma asked.

Dang, she would have to ask, Josh thought, reddening. The kids leaned in, eager for an answer.

"Ask me when you turn eighteen… maybe twenty-one," Josh said.

Winnie semi-whispered to Thelma. "Adult things." All four giggled.

"Hey!" Ben called out from the front. "Look at what's outside!"

All four children bolted through the swinging doors. "Wait up for me, kids!" Josh called to them, taking a picture of the bar.

Kit yelled. "Come join us, Uncle Josh! You've got to see this fog!"

Josh nearly dropped his cell phone. "Kids, get back in here!"

No reply.

He bolted for the door. Outside, the mist had enveloped the ghost town. "Winnie! Kit! Thelma! Ben!"

Nothing but silence answered from El Deseo. His nieces and nephews had vanished.

PANIC LAUNCHED AN all-out assault on Josh's chest. He was glad it only took three digits to type for help. But there was no signal. In fact, his cell phone was dead. Damn. He ran up and down the streets, calling for his nieces and nephews. All he could hear were echoes of his voice.

"Please don't be playing hide-and-seek!" His voice quivered. "It ain't funny!"

There was only silence in the cool morning mist. Buildings resembled shadows at the edge of town. *Wasn't it supposed to be 90 degrees in Southern New Mexico summers?*

He ran back the way they came, in case the kids started wandering home, though that wasn't their style. Halfway to the path, he noticed that it had widened and morphed into a graded road. *What the hell?*

Josh called the kids' names again. His red dri-fit shirt and shorts were soaked, worse than the time he attempted a 5k. Had they fallen into a mine shaft? They would all have to be unconscious, which meant a long drop. Had a bear or coyotes eaten them? Wouldn't there be screams? Had the most deadly predator... another human... silenced them? That would be the most terrifying outcome of all. He hadn't been to a church in years, but found himself on his knees praying they were just playing a prank on him.

The crunch of wood on gravel and stone brought him to his feet. Whatever it was, the sounds were headed his way. To his relief, it was a pair of cowboys on a buckboard, preceded by two horses clopping on the hardened trail at the edge of the mist. He bolted in their direction. These two reenactors could certainly help him.

"Hey guys!" He tried to sound natural, increasingly impossible with his rising panic. "Have you seen two young boys and two young girls roaming around out here?"

Both buckboard riders seemed to stare at him, looking at him up and down. Josh couldn't figure out if they were trying to assess his words or what he was wearing.

"Havin' kids run loose in these parts is a bad idea, Mister G," the driver spoke slowly.

Mr. G? He looked down at his red shirt. *Oh, the logo for the University of Georgia. It must not be very popular in Southern New Mexico.*

"Sorry... the kids ran off to check out the fog when my back was turned," he replied. "I'd appreciate it if you helped me look for them in this tourist spot."

Both gave him a hard stare from the top of the buckboard. "I don't rightly know what you're talking about, but if you have kids, you'd best gather them up and leave town fast, 'fore the Englishman gets 'em."

"Oh, okay… Englishman.…" Josh said in a mutter as they rode past him. "Got it." *Probably some new element to this ghost town, where they'd get rounded up and he'd have to pay a fee to get them loose. Could they do that?* He wished he had thought to bring his wallet on the morning walk.

HE HEADED BACK to El Deseo, a little less nervous now that there were others around. Even in the thick fog, he could see more people, reenactors by the looks of their period dress, moving about town. The Sunset Saloon was looking livelier. The Sheriff's office and jail, hotel, and mining office with the name "Haversham's" were bustling with activity. *When did all of these actors arrive? Did they arrive in the town, slipping past him in the fog?* His questions and pleas for help in searching for his kids were met with strange looks, no leads, and no offers of help. Most shied away from him as though he had COVID.

He glanced at the General Store and his jaw dropped. The walls and roof were fixed, and the place was doing a thriving business. They couldn't have rebuilt it that fast. Something was definitely wrong.

His chest pains increased. His heart raced, like the time his brother convinced him to do that 5k, and he woke up in an ambulance. In fact, his brother and sister and their significant others would be waking up right now. Would they go looking for him? Did he mention he was planning a ghost town hike when the adults played Cards Against Humanity after the kids went to bed? Would they remember it after all of those wine slushies? Would they even know where El Deseo was?

Something had changed in the fog. Was this what his Scoutmaster, Mr. Baugh, the Korean War veteran, had warned them about? How did the old man know the mist wasn't right?

Josh burst into the saloon, packed with card players and drinkers, most dressed as cowboys or in suits. Sprinkled about them were ladies in garish garments, a scene out of the history books that he used for teaching. One gal was on a swing, while another was just finishing a song to accompany the piano player.

Josh cupped his hands together. "Excuse me, folks, my name is Joshua Fletcher. Has anyone seen four small kids in modern clothes roaming around the town?"

Everything stopped, just like in the Western movies when a stranger walked through the swinging doors. All stayed quiet.

"Who wants to know?" said an older man in a clipped British accent behind him.

Josh spun around. "I do. They're mine."

He looked the old man over. Bowler hat, fancy suit and cravat, nice shoes, well-trimmed white beard, and a gleam in his eye that was more unsettling than friendly.

"You... are the father of all four?" The movement of his mouth revealed several golden teeth.

Josh glanced at the men in Western outfits gathering behind the old man. "Well, no, but I'm...."

The Englishman tapped his wooden cane with a metallic end that resembled a bullet on the planks of the saloon, the sound resembling the hammer of a judge's gavel. "Then they were orphans and now are legally my property."

Josh swallowed nervously. "They're my brother's and sister's kids, sir, not orphans."

The gold teeth reemerged in a smile. "You have proof of this?"

The history teacher didn't even have a wallet or car keys. "Not with me right now, but please, if they've done any damage, I'll pay you back later...."

The Englishman tapped his cane again, another legal pronouncement. "Sorry, Mister Fletcher, but they're just too valuable to me. Good day."

As he spun around, Josh flanked him and grabbed his lapels. "Please, sir, I'll gladly pay...."

The Englishman glanced over at one of the men with him, a star pinned to his vest. "Sheriff Roberts, this man is assaulting me. I believe a stay in jail is warranted now."

Several hands grabbed Josh and dragged him outside into the streets. His pleas went unheeded as they marched him off to the town's jail.

THIRTY MINUTES LATER the singer from the Sunset Saloon came over with one of the cowboys who had been playing cards at a table. She slid a warm biscuit between the jail bars, and what looked like a hunk of white cheese.

"I'm Molly Reilly, and I'm sorry about your kids," she offered. "The Englishman's taken children of Apache, Mexicans, immigrant kids, and orphans like yours."

"I'm Oscar Villalobos." The Hispanic cowboy held a wooden canteen up to the bars. Josh did his best to lap up a few swigs for his parched throat. He looked at the stained pan at the opposite side of the bench, a good idea of the accommodations. The sheriff seemed more engrossed in his solitaire game than with them.

"Won't he worry about what you might pass me?"

"Won't matter soon," Molly sighed, as if she knew what was coming.

"The Englishman uses the kids to squeeze into crevices to get more silver in the mine," Oscar said.

"It's cruel what he does to 'em," Molly said, a tear coming down, ruining her makeup.

Josh rattled the jail bars ineffectively. "Well, how can I get them back?"

Molly and Oscar each looked at each other. "Sometimes a father comes looking for his lost child," the singer replied.

"The Englishman gives him a choice. He can leave town and never return, without the child, or fight a duel with him at High Noon.

Josh sighed. "I take it his continued existence shows he always wins."

Molly nodded. "Did you see how many notches his cane had? He's trying to top Billy the Kid's record for most kills. He just needs one more to tie him."

The saloon singer looked Josh up and down. "I take it you're not a gunfighter."

Josh paced his cell, a jaguar in a cage. "I'm a history teacher."

Both looked worried. "The Englishman's quick on the draw," Oscar said. "You'll never get a shot off before he does."

Molly sat in the chair outside the jail. "Know any history that might help you survive this?"

Josh gave a nervous laugh. "I saw the play *Hamilton*, but the title character didn't do so well in that duel." Then his eyes bored into Molly. "Actually, I do have an idea."

JUST BEFORE NOON, the Englishman, the sheriff, and several men arrived at the jail. The leader's voice had that charming accent, but there was no warmth in the man's words.

"You can leave town alive at noon, childless, and never seek custody of those orphans again, or we can settle this with a gun duel. You beat me, and the children can leave with you."

Josh fixed him with a stare that seemed to have been forged by the blacksmith down the street. "We'll be having that duel at noon, sir."

The Englishman's eyes danced about merrily.

"But only if we use dueling pistols, not revolvers," Josh said.

The mine owner snapped his fingers, and an underling provided a box. The sheriff escorted Josh from the jail, where he inspected both pistols. Townspeople gathered along the streets to watch, though with the same enthusiasm as spectators at a game where one side was heavily favored.

"I thought I would bring a few new faces to our little duel." The Englishman waved his pistol toward the mining office. Sure enough, outside of Haversham's, he could see Winnie, Kit, Thelma, and Ben. All were chained at their wrists, faces grimy from a morning's work in the mine, no doubt. Bloody scrapes were visible on their faces, arms, and legs. Even Kit looked as terrified as the others.

"You'll pay for what you've done," Josh said in a mutter.

The two went to the center of the street, where the sheriff had marked off the paces. "Still time to back out, you know," the Englishman said airily. "You and your relatives can always make more kids. There's no reason for you to die today."

Josh gritted his teeth and shook his head. Then the two stood back-to-back. The sheriff began counting.

As soon as he said "twenty," Josh turned and caught a bullet in the chest. He flew a step backwards and collapsed on his back, eyes closed. The kids screamed for their uncle. Darkness came over him.

THE ENGLISHMAN CASUALLY handed his cane to an underling. "See that it gets another notch." Then he looked over at the sheriff. "Get a cart ready to give the body a ride up to Boot Hill. I had Mister Resnick dig a grave earlier this...."

"Look!"

Oscar's shouts led every eye to swing toward Josh, who was staggering to his feet, gasping, a whale beached on the shore, but nevertheless, still alive. He still clutched his dueling pistol.

"Uncle Josh!" the kids exclaimed in unison.

"That's impossible!" The Englishman's clipped accent became more of a scream. The townspeople gasped, murmurs of shock following. Though quivering, Joshua managed to stand erect.

"Now, it's my turn," he wheezed, sounding like a lifelong smoker.

The Englishman prepared to move, but Oscar called out. "Stand still, Mister Haversham. You know the rules."

A split second before Josh pulled the trigger, the Englishman dove to the side. The bullet whizzed where the mine owner had just stood.

"You cheated!" Molly screamed. "Everyone saw it!"

"Get him a new pistol and a second try!" the blacksmith shouted.

The Englishman got up, dusted himself off, and announced. "Mister Fletcher, you may now leave."

"Not without my kids!" Josh roared, wishing his gun had a second bullet.

"You've already got plenty of kids in that mine... you don't need four more!" a girl from the saloon shrieked.

The Englishman drew a small pistol from an ankle holster. "You should have left town when you had the chance, Mister Fletcher. I won't miss a second time."

Josh closed his eyes as a gunshot shattered the silence.

———————◆———————

HE OPENED HIS eyes. There was a giant red stain on the Englishman's chest. How....

The sheriff gasped. "Molly, what did you do?"

The saloon singer held the shotgun she had concealed under her shawl. "What I should have done the first time the Englishman sent a kid into the mine and killed his father trying to save him."

"Molly Reilly, I arrest you for the murder of William Haversham." Sheriff Roberts reached for his revolver, but his holster was empty. Oscar had taken it, and the pistol was now trained on him. "Take off that badge, Sheriff, and march out of town. You don't deserve it."

Still in shock, the lawman unpinned the star and tossed it into the street. Two of the Englishman's underlings drew guns, but many of the townspeople beat them to the punch. The pair laid down their weapons and joined the sheriff.

"Unlock those kids' chains," Molly commanded. "And get those other children out of the mine."

Guns pointed at them, the mining foreman and his men complied, urged on by Oscar. Unshackled, the kids bolted for their uncle, while Oscar urged the foreman into the mine. Within minutes, a diverse array of kids stumbled out of the giant hole where they had been forced to dig for silver.

The nieces and nephews hugged their uncle, slumped into the street, being attended by Molly and one of the other saloon girls.

"Dad... I mean Uncle Josh, what happened?" Winnie asked as the women had pulled off his red shirt. They saw their answer, as Molly unwound a slew of silks wrapped around his chest.

"It was your uncle's idea," Molly replied. "The girls and I brought him plenty of silks, but I never believed it would work."

Through gasps, Josh explained how a Tombstone physician used silks in the first-ever bulletproof vest. "It couldn't stop all guns, but it could block a dueling pistol shot, though I think the force of the shot broke a rib."

Thelma clasped her hands together while Kit looked at the silks. "You could have used a metal plate like that Clint Eastwood movie you showed us when our parents were out."

Josh smiled. "I thought about that, but reckoned he'd hear the clang and know something was up."

"There's a doctor coming toward us." Ben observed. He indicated a man with an apron and an array of metal tools that looked like Medieval torture devices.

"Uh, no thanks," Josh spoke rapidly. "I think we need to get through that mist and back to our own time."

When the townspeople gave him a look, Josh added "I mean, our own town."

Molly retrieved the star from the street and pinned it on Oscar. "I think you'll do a better job as El Deseo's new sheriff, Mister Villalobos," she said.

"And I think you'd be an even better mine owner than a singer," Oscar replied.

The girls from the saloon brought food over to the kids, who eagerly wolfed it down. Then the five said their goodbyes, though Josh could barely wave as they headed down the graded road, all walking hand-in-hand. As they passed through the mist, the trail narrowed to the dirt path, overgrown with weeds. Unfortunately, the pain in his chest persisted, and the kids still had their bloody scrapes. He'd have to come up with a story for his brother, sister, and their spouses, as they made their way toward their lodge.

Parents poured out of the cabin and hugged their children, while

the kids gave a symphony of stories about the Old West and their adventures. Their tales faced skepticism, but the parents provided hugs
and handkerchiefs, trying to wipe away the cuts and scrapes.

Josh smiled. "They had quite the adventure in that ghost town we
visited this morning, but if it's all the same to you, though, I'd prefer
Carlsbad Caverns."

Ivy emerged from the cabin. Josh stumbled up the stairs. Ignoring
the intense pain in his chest, he hugged her.

"Wow... what got into you?" She managed before he kissed her.

"I'm ready to be a husband and a father," he whispered in her ear.

THAT EVENING, IVY looked over at Josh. "Your proposal today at
lunch was sweet, and that gift shop ring was a nice touch. But why the
fire outside at night?"

Josh pulled a pair of sleeping bags from the car. "Gives us a little
more privacy from the lodge, my siblings, and the kids."

As she eagerly unrolled one of the sleeping bags, she glanced over
at her new fiancé. "Those were some pretty wild tales the kids told
over lunch, before you popped the question. What *really* happened?"

Josh pulled her toward him. "It'll cost you at least a kiss to get the truth."

She obliged, making it a good long one.

The history teacher smiled. "Okay, so I took the kids on a hike to the
ghost town of El Deseo, when this creepy fog came in and transported
us back to the 1800s."

She laughed. "You mean like this mist that's just now coming toward our campsite?"

Uh oh.

He broke free of her embrace in nanoseconds. "Ivy, throw our stuff
in the car!" Her curious look was met by a look of terror, urging her
on. He kicked sand over the flames. Already, he could hear whinnying
ponies and a gunshot or two, which made Ivy drop her questions and
jump into the shotgun seat.

As he revved the engine, he could make out the images of masked bandits on horseback, heading straight toward them. A bullet slammed into the rental station wagon.

"There goes our deposit," Ivy said as she ducked low.

"Not again!" he cried out as the vehicle sped away from their pursuers.

———————✦———————

—*John A. Tures began writing for the* El Paso Herald-Post *in high school. He wrote for his college paper at Trinity University in San Antonio and at Marquette University. He earned his doctorate at Florida State University, analyzed data in Washington D.C., and is now a Professor at LaGrange College. He writes a weekly column for newspapers and magazines. He has published a number of short story mysteries and thrillers. His book,* Branded, *will come out later this year with Huntsville Independent Press (Huntsville Independent Press). His author page is here: https://www.johntures.com/ about-the-author/. John would like to thank Beth, Asher, Zach, Jason and Sophia, along with Laura, Fred, Donna, Edna and Stella.*

Hunter by Alfred Jackob Miller

JUST ANOTHER DAY ON THE FARM

RIGO

THE SUNRISE WARMS a pleasant South Texas day in February. With his white hat pulled down over his leathered forehead to just above the thick gray eyebrows that ring his ninety-year-old eyes, Robert watches four hundred head of cattle from atop Hellfire, a mature black stud.

Beautiful morn', he thinks and unzips his gray, flannel-lined jacket, shifting his gaze to the nearest of the seven tanks on his five hundred acres where some of the herd lounge and drink. The rustling leaves of the pecan grove near his house catch his attention and he smiles at the sight of the sun just cresting his house. Sure as shit beats sortin' letters in a damn basement.

A cloud of dust rises on the horizon. Robert watches Jake's F-150 come into view, followed by the sound of tires crunching stone along FM 1717.

Taking the reins in the dark brown, wrinkled hand missing its ring finger, he tugs, and Hellfire turns to face the house.

"Jake musta left for town before dawn." Robert places his free hand on Hellfire's flank then nudges him with the heels of his muddy black boots.

Hellfire steps along the soft pasture toward the house, and the truck pulls into the drive, parking next to the well.

In a black suede jacket and black felt hat, Jake gets out of his truck. He leans against a post on Robert's porch, watching, his thumbs wedged between his jeans and leather belt, its large brass buckle polished to a shine.

"How do, *caballero viejo?*" Jake says as Robert steps down from Hellfire, his left leg buckling.

"Beautiful day. Any news from town, *vaquero?*" Robert leads Hellfire to the stable, hobbling as he walks, back bent.

"Same old!" Jake says as Robert disappears into the barn where he secures Hellfire, checks his trough, and feeds him a large carrot.

"Back soon, old boy." Robert strokes Hellfire's forehead.

Limping across the courtyard amidst his farmhouse, shed, and barns, Robert eyes the new Angus bull, Trompo. The brown mass of muscle tracks Robert's movement as he nears his pen.

Gotta clean your pen later. Then, out to stud with you.

"I don't like that bull," Jake says. "He's skittish. Where'd you get him?"

"Quit Sherlock Holmes'n."

Jake studies Robert's gait as he winces up the steps to his porch.

"Coffee?"

"Como no," Jake replies.

"I'll bring it out."

In the long, narrow kitchen, Robert pulls down a pair of mugs with chipped lips. He pours coffee from the half pot still warming on the percolator, adding two lumps of sugar to each. He brings the mugs out, setting them on the wicker table between the two rocking chairs. Grimacing, Robert lowers then drops into the chair, his back and leg popping.

Jake sips his coffee. "Mmm."

"No shit, mmm."

"Your one indulgence."

"This farm is an indulgence."

Jake laughs, then rubs his black mustache and sighs. "Our friends are worried about you. You're ninety, and your mobility ain't gettin' any better."

Robert puckers his lips and snorts in hard, rumbles up phlegm, and spits it into the grass. "My friends musta started a stitch and bitch group."

Jake laughs.

"This ain't beautiful mornin' conversation."

"Reckon it ain't, Robert."

"And I reckon I'll keep ranchin' 'til I fall and can't get up."

They sip coffee in silence for some time, watching the cattle graze.

"If you'd won the lotto, you think you'd still be ranching?"

Robert looks at the clouds passing. "You know the old joke."

"Yeah."

"Woulda kept ranchin' 'til I went broke again."

Both men smirk and nod.

"Figured you of all people'd understand, Jake, that I ain't fit for no old folks' home."

"No. You ain't."

THE SUN OVERHEAD and the day warm now, Trompo watches Robert approach the oval pen with a rusted wheelbarrow and shovel. Robert tugs his pants up, pulls at his silver belt buckle, and tightens it one notch against his taut waist.

"Jake's right. But we got to get acquainted," he says in a kind voice. The gate lock scrapes and clangs as Robert slides it open. Trompo spins to face him, the loose skin of his jowls jiggling.

"It's okay, big boy. I ain't like them that mistreated you." Robert steps inside and latches the gate closed, eyes on the bull. Trompo lowers his head and breathes out as the man pushes the wheelbarrow around the edge of the pen, approaching Trompo from his left. Shovel in hand, Robert scoops the piles of manure into the wheelbarrow until it's full. Dropping the shovel on top, he pushes the wheelbarrow to the gate, eyes on Trompo as he walks, his boots heavy now with mud.

"Nothin' to worry 'bout." He closes the gate and pushes the wheelbarrow toward the towering row of pecan trees where a chain-link fence encloses the big garden that lays fallow now. After dumping the manure in the corner, Robert returns to the bullpen where Trompo watches him work.

As the sun descends away from its apex, Robert's silver buckle catches the light and Trompo charges.

"Whoa!" Robert calls, dropping the shovel and turning to face the bull just in time to grab his horns before Trompo throws him back, spinning through the air. Robert lands on his knees and as he struggles to his feet, Trompo charges again.

"Shitfire," Robert says to himself, cursing his damaged back and leg. Still on one knee and gritting his teeth as Trompo nears, Robert dives perpendicular to the bull's charge. Trompo pivots and catches Robert above the belt buckle, driving his left horn deep, sending the man flying then crashing against an iron fencepost where he lays crumpled in a heap.

ROBERT EMERGES FROM the void, sprawled on his side, his left arm hanging across his chest, his right arm extended above his head. Mud weighs on his eyelashes as he blinks away the fog and spots Trompo eating hay fifty feet away on the far end of the pen.

With labored breathing, Robert takes in the smell of grass and the taste of manure in his mouth. He looks down at his torso where his shirt is covered in the shiny blackish blood that has mixed with mud in a puddle beside him.

Damnation. This my time of dyin'? Or another false alarm? He wiggles his toes and fingers, then registers the fencepost against his spine.

Gather your strength, viejo. He glances up and down the farm road, hoping to see a dust trail, but spotting none.

Closing his eyes, Robert remembers his first brush with death on the farm. It was a fine day in June, hot but dry with a refreshing breeze. The old red Ford tractor rumbled along under him, the steel seat tolerable back before his injuries. It had been a wet spring and the pasture grew more grass than his little herd of forty could eat. He steered the tractor back and forth across the sloped land like a slow metronome counting time in five-minute chunks, the hay baler working its magic behind him. Not far from the ditch beside the farm road the baler jammed, and Robert hopped down from the still-running tractor, heading back to inspect.

Probably the slip clutch, he thought as he trudged across damp earth, remembering the instructions his neighbor gave him. *Nope. Ain't nothin' broke. This here stretch of grass at the bottom of the hill is just too wet.* He knelt to inspect the clumpy grass at the front end of the seven-by-seven foot cube-shaped machine. There, he spotted a big stone amidst the pegs on the long pickup rail, the cylinder that cut and pulled grass into the machine.

"Ah," he said and headed to the control panel on the side of the machine to turn it off.

With a crowbar from the tractor, Robert pried out the rock and tossed it over the fence where it thudded a few feet from the road. He restarted the machine, and it rumbled to life with the smell of gas filling his nostrils as the engine exhaled a puff of black smoke.

He knelt down to inspect the pickup reel, finding the cylinder spinning, then reached in front of the spinning teeth to pull away clumps of wet grass that fell out with the stone. Crawling forward, the wind from the cylinder blowing against his face, his right knee slipped on a rock and his body shifted toward the machine. The hungry teeth of the pickup reel latched onto his ring finger and shirtsleeve, the finger popping free at the knuckle, disappearing into the whirl of steel and grass.

Blood spurted as the cylinder pulled Robert's shirt, his boot digging into the soil. Gritting his teeth, he saw an image of the machine mashing his body like a meat grinder. Robert fought with all his strength until the shirt tore at the cuff, and he launched back as the stitching separated.

Laying on his back, looking at the clouds passing overhead, he heard a whisper, but couldn't make out the words with the tractor and baler growling so close.

STILL ON HIS side, bleeding to death, Robert slides down, reaching for the fencepost, his belt picking up mud and pebbles as he scrapes along the earth. Trompo's ears flicker, and he spins toward the sound.

The bull faces him, head lowered. He grunts and lifts his back right hoof.

Now. Robert reaches for the lowest iron beam of the fence with his right hand and pulls himself, pushing with his boots and rolling away from the charging bull, wincing as he passes over his stomach then onto his right side again.

Trompo skids to a stop, splattering mud. Robert closes his eyes, his head spinning from the effort. After a deep breath, he looks down at his gut.

Am I bleeding less, or just running out of blood? His face contorts into a half-smile.

Time to make the call. He lifts his left hand to his mouth, inserts his index finger and thumb, then blows a piercing whistle. Hellfire answers with a neigh and a kick to the stable door.

Robert relaxes, remembering another of his brushes with death.

"Wild and vicious bastard," Jake said to his friends seated at the corner table in the busy café in the county seat. "Lookin' like I'll have to put him down."

"Can't sell him?" someone asked.

Jake shook his head. "Won't let nobody examine him."

"Did you buy him sight unseen?" another man asked, sipping his coffee.

"Shit no. Someone gave him to me. Same as I'm trying to pawn him off on one of you."

The friends laughed.

"Knew you didn't have the heart to put a horse down," Robert said.

"You fellas would do the same if you was in my boots," Jake said.

"Sure as shit would," one of the men said, making them all laugh again.

"I'll take him," Robert said, then elbowed Jake. "You can come over and enjoy the horse ribs I'll barbecue."

"Shit. You'd be the last of us to put a horse down," Jake replied.

Two days later, defying his eighty-year-old body, Robert climbed up on the wild-eyed black stallion in the narrow stock chute outside the round pen on Jake's ranch. The horse tried to buck him right away, and Robert held onto the saddle with one hand and the fencing of the stock chute with the other.

"Ready?" Jake asked, his hand on the latch to open the gate.

Robert shook his head and climbed off, the horse thrashing beneath him. "This horse is angry. Like he's filled with the fires of hell. Reckon he was abused. Let's bring him to my farm. Let him settle in my stables and see if I can't earn his trust."

Thus began a regimen of apples and carrots, sweet talk, and daily trots around the corral that abutted the stable, and then one day, Hellfire let Robert brush him. Soon after, he let Robert rub him between the eyes. A couple weeks later, with Jake perched on the fence of the corral watching, Robert saddled Hellfire and mounted him.

He rubbed the majestic horse on his shiny black flank. "You're okay, boy."

Then, Hellfire bolted, kicking and bucking and, after a few seconds, sent Robert careening into the steel fence.

Broken leg, broken back.

But then, the horse walked over and sniffed at Robert while Jake called 9-1-1.

After six months of recovery, and more of the daily regimen of apples and carrots, brushing, and sweet talk, Robert mounted him again.

"You're the world's stubbornest *caballero*," Jake said, watching, perched on the corral fence.

This time, Hellfire let Robert lead him around the pen. No bucking, no bolting, though twice he bit at Jake when Robert rode him too close.

"Mean bastard," Jake said under his breath.

"He was testin' me," Robert said later. "To see if I'd turn on him. Bet we'll be *simpatico* now."

"El triunfo del coraje."

Robert shrugged. "Just another day on the farm."

THE POUNDING OF steel-clad hooves on wood continues as Robert bleeds onto the mud and Trompo chews his hay.

Moseying like this kingdom is yours. Robert glances toward the stables where the pounding continues. *You can do it, Hellfire.*

Then comes the sound of the stable door clanging open, and Hellfire gallops out of the barn straight to Robert, lowering his muzzle to the man's face.

"We've done this before," he says. "You 'member? 'Cept this time it'll be bareback."

Hellfire breathes out of his nose, sending a blast of hot air over Robert's face along with the scent of spring and grass.

"Give me a minute."

Robert closes his eyes remembering the hot August day he was tending his garden with a shovel and hoe under the shade of his pecan trees.

The tomatoes were plump and orange and above him hung an enormous crop of pecans. Hellfire was tethered to a tree nearby. As Robert picked up his thermos of ice water, Hellfire whinnied then stood on his hind legs, kicking at the air.

"What is it old—ah!" Robert cried at a feeling like thorns puncturing, then tearing, at his left calf. Then again on his right heel. He turned and spotted one thick red and orange copperhead slithering away under the garden fence. Another copperhead, brown and dark red, with an enormous head, was lodged in the heel of his right boot, its fangs still pumping venom into his body.

"Dios mio," Robert whispered, a burning sensation climbing his calves. He reached for the shovel where it rested against the fence, raised it up, then drove the blade down on the snake's neck. Head severed, he pried it out with the shovel blade, removing the fangs from his heel. Using the shovel for support, he staggered to Hellfire, loosened the reins from the tree, climbed on his back, then passed out.

He came to in a hospital hours later. Jake, black felt hat in his hands, sat in a chair by the bed, standing when Robert's eyes fluttered open.

"Lucky *pendejo viejo*," Jake said, smiling. "Hellfire brought you to my place, then bit me on the ass when I hauled you down."

"Where is he?"

"I brought you to the hospital then went back. Distracted him with a bucket of apples and managed to tie the devil to a fencepost."

"Smart."

"Reckon Hellfire paid back his debt to you today."

"We're even."

ROBERT TAKES ANOTHER deep breath. You ain't gettin' any younger, and you're a dead duck if you just lay here bleedin'.

With the force of will left in his ninety-year-old body, Robert pushes himself up to his knees, raises one foot, then the other, standing, and taking hold of Hellfire as he lowers his head.

How am I going to get up in this state? No saddle, no stirrups.

"Steady yourself, boy," he says and takes hold of Hellfire's mane in his left hand, pulling as Hellfire pushes Robert up with his head. Robert lifts his right leg, almost getting the heel of his boot onto Hellfire's back. But then his body gives out and he plummets to the ground on his left side.

Trompo snorts.

Robert looks at the sky and at Hellfire, who sniffs at Robert's head. "End of the road, old boy. Unless someone stops by or you get it in your head to go to Jake's."

Smiling at his horse, Robert sees himself in the mailroom he worked for ten years before he bought the farm. "Woulda been easy to stay at the post office. Job security. Benefits. But I was dyin' there, one sorted letter at a time. Needed to breathe the open air. Be master of my fate."

He closes his eyes, remembering the shitty nursing home where his father died sipping water from a straw, feeling those paint-chipped walls closing in.

"Nope," he says in a whisper, his vision blurring. "This is a good death."

Hellfire stands over him like a sentinel.

"But what will become of you, *amigo?* Jake," he says. "Hellfire. Go for Jake."

Hellfire sniffs at Robert.

"Go—" Robert's throat catches. "Hellfire."

His body shutting down, Robert persists for what feels like an eternity, outside of time, vivid memories playing through his mind, until he hears a whisper on the wind, making out the words this time. "Hellfire," he murmurs with his last breath.

———————————

— *Originally from Texas, Rigo lives in Amherst, Massachusetts with his family. His creative writing has appeared in* Syncopation Literary Journal, THEMA, Middleground Magazine, *and* A Thin Slice of Anxiety.

A mixed-race visual artist, multi-instrumentalist, and singer-songwriter, Rigo is querying a number of novel-length works, is a member of the rock band Black Door '74 (https://blackdoor74band.com/), and also performs music solo (www.rigoartist.com). Facebook: https://www.facebook.com/profile. php?id=100011288868620

DROP THAT RIFLE

M.F. McDONNELL

THE ONLY SOUND was the snorting breath of his flagging horse and the gritty crunch of the hooves striking the sandy, rock-strewn ground. He reached back for his saddlebags. If he lost those, he had lost everything. As Palmer crested a the low ridge, he looked back over his shoulder. He could not see them, but he knew they were there. Somewhere behind a hill or hidden in the dust, they were there.

Slowing to a walk he headed into the cottonwoods and brush that lined a narrow stream trickling through an arroyo. If he could lose himself until the sun set, they might not find him in the dark.

His horse was likely beyond saving. He debated in his mind whether to kill the animal. If he did so, he might very well perish carrying the heavy saddlebags himself in the heat, but he was not about to leave the bags behind.

A small voice said, "Mister, are you okay?"

On the far side of the stream stood a boy, no more than eight years of age, holding a pail. The boy had a soft, high-pitched voice with an accent that made the word sound like *'mist-ah.'*

The boy could not be alone. "Where are your people, son?" Palmer's hand hovered near his holster, ready to kill if he had to.

"Over there." The boy pointed through the trees. "What's wrong with your horse? It looks–" the boy began, but Palmer interrupted him.

"Take me to them," he said.

The boy was frightened by the man's gruff tone and suffering horse. But his father had taught him, even at such a young age, not to show fear.

"I have to get water for my ma." The boy stepped toward the creek.

"I said take me to your parents, boy. Now you listen to me," Palmer said in a growl.

"You listen to me," said another voice, startling Palmer. He almost drew his Colt but stopped himself as a man appeared out of the brush. "You will not speak to my son in such a manner."

A pistol was holstered on the man's hip, and he carried an old, but cared for, Henry repeating rifle.

"My apologies, sir." Palmer needed to determine his situation before deciding what to do about it. "I didn't mean to scare the boy, but...."

"You don't scare me," said the boy. His father looked at him proudly.

Palmer wanted to tell the boy not to interrupt his elders but was aware that would not help matters.

"Again, my apologies. I'm tired and hungry which is making me out of sorts."

The man noticed the unfriendly way Palmer looked at him.

"Your horse, your business," said the man, aware now that the dirty, tired man facing him was frightened. Despite a growing trepidation, the man was a gentleman.

"My name is Hogan. John Hogan. This is my son Jacob. We're just about to have supper. You may join us if you wish. But perhaps you need to tend to your horse."

Palmer, wary of who he might be joining, ignored the last comment. He was in bad need of food and coffee.

The boy filled the bucket before he and his father walked away through the cottonwoods. The father tried to take the pail, but the lad refused him. Water slopped down the boy's pant legs as he walked.

Leaving his horse tied to some branches so that it might reach both grass and water, Palmer followed the man and boy. He had, for the moment, forgotten about those who followed him. His concern now was with those in front of him.

In the shade of the trees was a Conestoga wagon. A team of oxen grazed nearby, alongside a single horse. A woman stirring a pot over a small fire straightened as the men approached. A loose-fitting dress indicated she had not been eating properly. Palmer looked again at Hogan and realized that neither the woman nor her husband had been eating enough. Only the boy appeared well-fed.

"This is my wife, Sandra." Hogan turned to Palmer. "I don't know your name, sir."

Palmer thought quickly.

"It's Coppins. Pleased to make your acquaintance, ma'am," Palmer lied politely.

"I'm pleased to meet you, Mister Coppins. You'll join us for supper?"

"My friends call me Charlie," Palmer said. "I'd like it if you all would call me that."

Palmer was lying through his teeth with every word.

A small table and three kitchen chairs had been set up on the sandy ground. Young Jacob struggled to get a fourth chair from the wagon. Neither of his parents moved to help him. Palmer realized the boy was being raised to be self-reliant. Jacob finally dropped the chair from the wagon and dragged it to the table.

As they sat down to dinner, Palmer eyed the Hogan's horse. His own was as good as dead. This would be a perfect replacement.

Palmer was trying his best to be friendly while plotting in his mind. "You folks have come over the trail alone?" he asked.

"We have. Part of the way. A disagreement at Fort Union among the others caused us to leave the train. That was almost a fortnight ago." Hogan spoke with the same accent as his son. He pronounced the word 'fawtnight'.

"Where are you bound?" Palmer asked.

The woman responded, "Santa Fe. We're joining my brother and his family."

"And where are you from, if you don't mind the intrusion?"

"Originally from Connecticut. We tried homesteading in Ohio before Sandra's brother offered us to partner on his ranch. We've been on the trail almost four months now. The trouble at Fort Union held us up, of course."

"How much further to Santa Fe, Mister Coppins?" asked the woman.

"You're likely looking at another week or more." Palmer continued his lies. "You may wish to rest here for a spell before making the climb over the mesa at Glorieta."

Palmer made it sound as if the Glorieta Pass was barely surmountable. In truth, the trail was good and not too steep. They were no more than two days travel from Santa Fe.

"What does your brother do, if you don't mind my asking?" said Palmer.

"He has a ranch," said Hogan. "Corbett's place. Would you happen to know of it?"

It took all Palmer's will to hide his emotions. "I'm not familiar with the name, but I'm only passing through," he lied.

"Thank you for the stew, ma'am," Palmer said abruptly. "Those were fine biscuits. If you'll excuse me, I want to check on my horse."

He found his horse dead lying on its side.

Struggling to pull the rifle and saddlebags from under the horse's weight, he was unable to do so. He tried to control himself. The news that these people were heading to the very place he had left a day earlier was shocking.

Walking back into the camp, he announced sadly, "My horse is dying. It's laying on the rifle scabbard. Would you be so kind as to lend me your rifle? I can't let him suffer."

Hogan looked at him angrily. "Why did you ride that animal so hard? What are you running from that made you do that?" he demanded.

"It was the mountains that did it, sir. The horse couldn't stand the strain. May I borrow your rifle?" Palmer asked again.

"Jacob, you stay with your mother. I'll help Mister Coppins."

The two men walked into the cottonwoods leaving mother and son watching them.

Palmer led the way through the trees and scrub brush. He turned suddenly, viciously striking Hogan on the forehead with the butt of his pistol. Hogan silently collapsed onto the sandy ground.

Palmer knew he had to move quickly. He picked up the rifle that Hogan had dropped and strode back to the campsite.

"Where's John?" Sandra asked.

"He's indisposed, ma'am." Palmer smiled at her. "I'm going to need to take that horse of yours. And I may take something else of yours while I'm at it." He laughed.

Sandra Hogan had learned many things on the Santa Fe Trail. One of those things was to trust no one. She had been wary of Palmer the minute she laid eyes on him and had prepared accordingly.

"Indisposed how? What have you done with my husband," she asked with a calmness she didn't feel.

"Never you mind about that. I need your help to move my horse. Come with me." He looked around the camp. "Where's the boy? Jacob, where is he?"

When he turned back to the woman she was pointing a pistol at his chest. No more than ten feet from him. She could hardly miss if she fired.

Palmer held the rifle with his right hand gripping the receiver. To fire, he'd need to change his grip and action the lever or drop the rifle and go for his pistol.

"Mister, you put down that rifle right now," said a small voice.

Palmer turned his head to find Jacob pointing his father's pistol with both hands. The hammer was cocked and ready to fire, and the gun was shaking in the boy's small hands.

"Jacob, be careful," said his mother.

Palmer laughed. The kid had the jump on him. If he could be outsmarted by a mother and child, he didn't deserve to live.

Ignoring the woman, he turned slowly to face Jacob.

"Boy, put down the gun before someone gets hurt. You misunderstand what's happening."

"My pa is dead down by the river. This man hit pa in the head," he said to his mother, "and he's bleeding bad."

"Drop that rifle right now," the boy said to Palmer.

Palmer found it humorous that this small boy was using the words of an adult but spoke with the high-pitched voice of a child.

"Drop it," said Sandra Hogan. "You can't beat both of us."

Palmer hesitated, glancing sideways to see the woman with her pistol still trained at his chest.

"Perhaps not, but I can kill your boy before you kill me. Is that what you want?"

The bullet struck Palmer in the right shoulder, shattering his collar bone. The rifle fell from his hand as he dropped to his knees. Unable to move his right arm, he fumbled with his left hand, trying to draw across his body. The woman fired, striking him in the center of his chest. He flopped down on his face in the sand.

"Jacob." She cried running to her son. She took the pistol from his hands and hugged him. "Where's your father?"

"In the bush over there." He pointed. Looking wide-eyed at Palmer he asked, "Is he dead, ma? Did I kill him?"

"Jacob, you are very brave. Very brave. He won't hurt us now. Let's find your father."

With the three pistols tucked into her apron sash and carrying the rifle she followed Jacob to her husband.

They found Hogan struggling to get up. Blood ran down his face, presenting a horrifying sight for young Jacob. The boy, however, stood his ground.

"I heard gunshots," John Hogan said, mumbling while wiping blood from his vacant eyes.

"Yes, John. Thanks to Jacob, our valiant little man. He saved my life."

They heard the soft *thud* of horse's hooves on sand and looked up to see several men riding to them. The lead man, much to her surprise, was her brother.

"Sandra, good Lord, is it you? What's happened? We heard shots." Her brother stepped off his horse and hugged her.

"Look here, Mister Corbett," said one of the men with her brother. "These are our saddlebags." It took three men to lift the horse enough to recover the saddlebags, the rifle, and the saddle.

Two of the men led an insensible and very unsteady John Hogan back to the camp.

"That's Drew Palmer, all right," said one of the men after they had rolled Palmer's body over. "Murderer, thief, and liar."

"He told us his name was Coppins," Sandra said.

Another of the hands laughed and said, "I'm Charlie Coppins. The rounder stole my name as well as the money."

"Palmer worked for me," Corbett said. "He killed my lead hand and made off with our payroll money. We followed him here. You're lucky. He's ruthless. You shot him twice?" he asked Sandra.

"Jacob wounded him in the shoulder. My shot is in his chest."

"Jacob?" Corbett said excitedly. "Why, my nephew is quite a hero."

Jacob was nowhere in sight. One of the ranch hands found him by the stream curled into a ball and crying.

Corbett sat down beside the boy. "We've never met, but your ma has written me many letters telling me all about you. You're a very brave boy. I guess we need to stop calling you a boy. You're a young man now. You understand what I'm telling you, Jacob? You saved three lives today, including your own."

"Yes, sir," Jacob said with a sniffle. "I guess I understand."

"Your pa will explain it to you better, but he's hurt right now. He'll be okay, though. He just needs to rest a spell."

"Yes, sir."

"Call me Uncle Jake, if you would."

"Jake. That's my name," said the boy.

"You're named after me, son. Your ma did that and I am honored. I wish I was as brave as you are. When you get a bit older, you're going to be a great help around my place."

"Yes, sir, Uncle Jake. I can help you. Pa tells me all the time how much help I am to him and Ma."

Jake Corbett put his arm around his nephew and almost cried he was so proud of the boy. "Then let's go help your mother."

"Yes, sir. I like helping. Ma's been teaching me how to cook. She says a man can't expect a woman to always be around to cook for him."

Jake Corbett laughed long and hard.

"Well, son, your ma and me had the same mother. That's exactly what our ma said to me when I was a youngster. Seems your ma was paying attention. Let's go see what help she needs right now."

———※———

—M. F. McDonnell is an emerging Canadian author from Waterford, Ontario. New to writing fiction, his short story "Thirst" was published in Under the Hot Prairie Sun *in April, 2025. "Heroes of a Sort", was published in May 2025 at close2thebone.co.uk. His short story "Good Riddance" was published in* Aces, Eights, and Unmarked Graves *in August. In addition to writing further short stories, he is currently completing work on a novel.*

THE DEBT

DR. REBECCA FOSTER

JESSUP JOHNSON'S HEAD ached. Slowly, he rose off the bedroom floor. The room spun as waves of nausea threatened to overtake him. He barely made it to bed before passing out. It's no wonder I'm starving, he thought as the sun was showing past noon. Jessup's aching head, blurry vision, along with a downright fuzzy memory wasn't helping either.

"Liv," he said, "Hon, will you fix me a steak and fry up a couple of taters? Is there any coffee? My head is killing me. My stomach is rumbling."

As Jessup washed, he noticed scratches on his fists and a sore spot on the side of his head. Livvy would fix him a nice steak, like she always did, when he had been out late playing cards and drinking.

I must have really wandered in like a bear last night, he thought as he surveyed the damages in the kitchen. Livvy's China plates, she had before they married, lay in shards scattered on the floor, chairs tumbled into heaps, her favorite shawl covered in blood and torn. Jessup had a sinking feeling he had overstepped himself. However, even at his worst he knew he would never have laid a hand on Liv in anger. He stared at the mess as bits and pieces of the night began to fall into place. He remembered Liv's scream woke him, and he ran to the edge of the kitchen. He remembered hitting someone. But nothing else. Only darkness filled his head.

A feeling of urgency overtook him as he searched the barn and checked the corral for her horse. Gone. Buttercup, her saddle, and Liv were gone. *It looks like wherever she went, Liv didn't go willingly.* The dirt was kicked up near the corral gate, and a torn piece of her dress was hung on a post splinter.

From the house, he grabbed cold biscuits, sliced ham, a couple tins of peaches, a rifle, extra shells, and a bed roll. Outside once again, he spotted their tracks. The two riders and Buttercup trailed to the southeast. The direction they headed was near his brother's house. Jessup knew he would need JJ's help.

JJ, or Jeremiah Johnson, was a hulk of a man whose military training could help them find Liv. He had fought in several Indian uprisings and was a decorated soldier. After the military, he came to stay with Jessup and Liv while he built his house. He and Kelly were introduced by a friend and married soon afterwards.

JJ and Kelly gathered supplies as Jessup relayed what he could remember of last night. Kelly gave Jessup a hug, kissed her husband, and the two brothers were off. It didn't take long to find the trail of Buttercup and the other two horses. One of Buttercup's shoes had a slight cut in the inside edge. Jessup was supposed to have her reshod. Now, he was grateful he hadn't, the cut in the shoe made tracking her easier. It took some convincing for JJ to get Jessup to stop, eat, and sleep. Finally asking, "Would you rather miss the trail and wander off wasting time?" Jessup knew his brother was right, and the horses needed rest too.

As they dismounted, JJ noticed a drop of dried blood on Jessup's ear. "Let me look at your head. ... Well, Jessup, your head must be harder than rock. No wonder you don't remember anything. Someone dented your head with a pistol butt. Can't remember what happened if you're out cold."

Now it made sense. He remembered hitting someone and hearing them crash to the floor. He also remembered seeing another man with a scar on his face. A sigh of relief eased his heart knowing he had not hurt Liv. Yet in the same thought, he pitied the men who had stolen her.

LIVVY

LIV, TIRED FROM riding, was thankful she hadn't been hurt. Well, except for the fight she put up in the house and round two at the corral, she only had a few sore spots.

She studied the two characters. Bill was the brains of the bunch as he did most of the talking. He was thinner and shorter with a neater trim to his hair, mustache, and beard. Tom was the muscle of the group. She instinctively thought it would be unwise to cross him. He seemed unkempt with red hair, tan skin, and a scar over his left eye. He spoke very little when a nod or shake of his head would suffice as an answer. She was worried about Jessup. For a flicker of a second, she felt pity for Bill and Tom when Jessup caught up with them. The events of last night replayed in her head.

Liv had wrapped her shawl around her as she heard footsteps on the porch. Jessup was already asleep. She opened the door expecting something was wrong with JJ or Kelly. Two men pushed their way into the house. Liv screamed for Jessup. Grappling for her, they managed only to tear off part of her shawl. Jessup came from the bedroom, saw what was going on, and slugged the thinner man closest to him. The force of the hit caused the man to go down with a thud. His body hit hard against the table triggering the dishes to cascade to the floor. With quick strides, the second man crossed the floor and brought his pistol down on Jessup's head. Jessup fell backwards, landing on the bedroom floor motionless. Liv ran to his side and sopped up the oozing blood with the remaining parts of her shawl. The two men grabbed at her as she darted around them, toppling a chair. They were too much for her to fight as they shoved her toward the doorway. The force sent her tumbling off the porch, landing in the dirt with a loud, "oof." The men had their hands on her before she could regain her footing, pulling her toward the corral.

"Just you listen, you wild cat. Tom has no problem with going in and finishing off your man, then tying you across your horse. Or you can climb on it right now, and we will leave." Bill's face was stern as he spoke to her.

Liv knew it was fruitless to fight. Probably better to take a chance on escape given they threatened to go back in and shoot Jessup. Reluctantly, she mounted Buttercup.

"That's more like it." To emphasize his point, Bill gave her another harsh stare.

It seemed they traveled forever before stopping. Liv was grateful for the cool stream to wash some of the dust off and rest for a moment. Bill and Tom took turns keeping an eye on her and someone always held a rope on her horse as they traveled. For the most part, she ignored their questions and attempts for conversation. They gave her a blanket, tied one of her legs to Bill's leg with a short span of rope. "So, you don't get it in your mind to run off during the night."

Liv hadn't cried yet. Every time the tears welled up she coughed, choking them back down—determined she was not about to show any signs of weakness. Looking at the stars, she hoped Jessup was safe. She had no doubt he would come for her. She had to wait.

JESSUP

JESSUP LOOKED AT the stars and hoped Liv was unharmed. He also hoped she knew demons, or even the gates of hell, would not stop him from getting her back by his side. He slowly drifted off thinking she would be in his arms soon.

Morning came too quickly. As JJ made coffee, they shared biscuits with ham. The two were already mounted as soon as the sun broke over the edge of the hill. They wasted no time getting back on the trail. By noon, they found where the group had watered horses and camped for the night. They were making progress to catch up with them. Once in a while a drift of dust could be seen in the far distance.

LIVVY

"WHY DID YOU take me? I have never seen either of you. We have not even met."

Bill chose his words carefully as he responded, "We have not met formally, ma'am, it's true. Tom and I were crossing your land, umm—one step ahead of a posse—which was a misunderstanding on their part, and I caught a glimpse of you sitting on your porch. Pretty as a picture."

He paused. "Well, you see, then several months later we got into some gambling trouble on this boat in New Orleans. So, I told the captain about you, and I bet him you would make a wonderful companion during those long weeks at sea. He agreed to cancel our debt if I would deliver you to him."

The shock and disgust shone brightly on her face. It took a few minutes to find her voice. "So, I am payment for your debt. How much am I worth?" she tentatively asked.

"Three hundred dollars. Cash on the barrelhead." Bill grinned.

"I would rather jump in the sea, drown, and be eaten by fish. I have a husband and family who care for me. What makes you think I would agree to be a part of this... this nonsense?" Liv turned sharply and sat down on the nearest rock.

Her comment perplexed both Bill and Tom at first. They hadn't thought she would refuse their idea. They had considered her to be upset but not a refusal. To them it was simple—find someone to please the captain and it would free them from debt. She happened to be an easy means for a quick solution.

Her brain screamed trying to process what she had learned. *New Orleans, selling me into service to a Captain, for a three-hundred-dollar gambling debt!* Liv's lip quivered, and her eyes almost gave way to the tears. *Jessup where are you?*

JESSUP

"I KNOW THE trail must be here. It's gotta' be here. JJ, I can't lose her. I can feel her getting farther and farther away."

"Okay, let's back track to where they went into the rockslide and see if we can catch a glimpse of horseshoe scuffs on the rocks. We will find them."

What seemed like hours of searching for the slightest glimmer finally paid off, and once again, they were on the right path.

Liv, darling where are you?

LIVVY

IT WAS EVENING when they reached New Orleans. Liv had almost given up hope of Jessup finding her. Tom took care of getting the horses fed and bedded down for the night. Bill arranged and paid for two rooms above the saloon. One room for Tom, and one for Bill and Liv to share.

"You take the bed, and I'll sleep on my bedroll by the door," he said when a panicked look crossed her face. He paid one of the saloon girls to find Liv a suitable dress, saying Liv wasn't feeling well and needed to rest. Keeping her dignity intact, he gave Liv the privacy of a hot bath.

"Tomorrow, you need to look your best." He grinned as he closed and locked the door.

She could hear his boots pacing the hallway outside and occasionally listening at the door. Seeing no way to escape, Liv's hope faded. Worry and exhaustion set in as she finally closed her eyes and slept.

JESSUP

JESSUP AND JJ arrived in New Orleans before suppertime the next evening. Despite being tired, the determination to have Liv back in his arms kept Jessup going.

"JJ, let's check the livery stables for Buttercup. Looks like there is one at the beginning of town and one at the end. You take the right side of the street at the beginning, and I'll take the left side. We can meet up at the saloon at the far edge."

"Sounds good," JJ answered.

Both men checked the stables and the horses tied out front of the buildings hoping to catch a glimpse of Buttercup. It was the stable at the far end of town where Jessup found Liv's horse. Buttercup was patiently eating her oats and hay. She looked to be in good shape, so Jessup took this as a good sign for Liv as well. He didn't ask the livery owner about the horse, no need to raise any suspicions. Having no idea who had taken Liv, the less people who knew why they were there, the better it would be for her. Excitedly, he strolled a couple of doors down to the saloon so he could meet up with JJ. JJ was sitting at a table with his back to the wall and had already ordered their dinner. Jessup sat down across from his brother.

"I found Buttercup."

"Didn't you say one of the guys was large and one was thin?"

"Yep, best as I recall. The larger one had a scar over his eye. I saw it as he was bringing his gun down on my head before my lights went out."

"Think I may have seen him. He came down, ate, and then went back upstairs. Within a few minutes, a thin guy came down, ate, and then asked for a plate of food to take to his 'wife' who was ailing." Jessup's body slumped, listening to the words JJ spoke. What if they had come all this way and it wasn't her. Before he could say anything else, their thoughts were interrupted by the squeak of the saloon doors.

An older gentleman walked in and sat down at a table near the stairs. A few minutes later the thin man joined him. They exchanged pleasantries. The thin gentlemen's eyes darted around as they spoke. The brothers were too far away to catch much of the conversation, occasionally a word or two would drift their way. The best they could piece together was the older man was a captain on a gambling boat and something about debt and girl. The two men shook hands and walked up stairs.

LIVVY

LIV PULLED A blanket up to her neck. Although she was fully dressed, she did not like the way the captain was leering at her.

Then he spoke, "Ma'am, I am Captain Mac Martin at your service. Well, Bill, she sure is feisty and better looking than what you promised. When are we going to get her to my ship?"

"I figure later tonight when the town settles down. This way the saloon boss won't try and stop her leaving. Tom and I can escort her out the door and straight into your arms."

"Yep, she'll do fine. Right fine. See you at midnight." He grinned. The two men shook hands again. The captain stopped with his hand on the door. "Oh, and if for some reason you don't show up with the girl, I promise neither of you will make it out of New Orleans... alive." This chilling warning was delivered with such calmness it caused the hairs on the back of Bill's neck to rise.

After the door closed, Liv turned three shades of red, bounded off the bed, and slapped Bill hard across the face. He drew a deep breath and caught Liv unprepared for the slap he returned to her. Grabbing her solidly around the shoulders with a low sneer he told her, "Never lay your hands on me again or by the time Tom finishes with you, your own mother won't be able to recognize who you are." He had already threatened her about staying silent when the captain came upstairs. The slap she received banished any doubts of the level of evil to which these two would stoop.

Liv sat back down on the side of the bed with her back to them. Although her cheek was stinging, and she had sworn not to cry, a few tears fell onto her lap. She heard Bill talking to Tom. "I have been hinting to the saloon girls that my 'wife' was sickly. Naturally, if she needed the doctor, we would have to carry her out."

JESSUP

JJ TOOK A deep breath as the captain walked down the stairs and out the doors.

Jessup started to rise to his feet as they watched the captain leave. "Let's go get Liv."

"What's your plan? What are you going to do, barge through every door until you see her—if we even have the right men? Maybe get shot in the process of bustin' down doors."

"Um, yeah. You got a better plan?"

"Listen, little brother, for Liv's safety, we gotta think first and then act. We are not sure she is even up there. We wait, watch, and plan. Besides, we gotta eat."

Finishing up the last bites of apple pie, they were interrupted with movement on the stairs. The larger man had a blanket thrown over his shoulder covering a body, and the thin man was right behind them. JJ and Jessup watched the figures descend the steps. The body was small framed and wisps of auburn colored hair tumbled out of the edge of the blanket. With one quick movement, JJ scooted his chair over and grabbed Jessup's arm pinning him to the chair.

He said in a low voice, "Not here." They both knew it was Livvy.

One of the saloon girls met them at the end of the stairs, "Bill, oh, your wife is still ailing, I see?"

"Yes, we are headed over to Doc's office now. Thanks for your help with the food and dress." He flashed her his brightest smile. She gave a brief nod and went back to serving customers. Jessup bristled at the thought of Liv being sick or hurt on account of these scoundrels. The two men and their bundle gave a shove to the swinging doors and headed toward the livery.

Once inside the stables out of view, they sat Liv down, pulled the gag out of her mouth, then untied her hands and feet. Jessup and JJ kept a safe distance as the three riders headed out of town.

LIVVY

THE TIME SPENT riding through town and out to the waterfront felt like an eternity. Liv had been reminded of Bill's warning of her fate in Tom's hand before they left the livery.

Right on cue, Tom acknowledged the warning with a crooked toothed grin and a nod. She kept her head down and didn't dare look at anyone to give the appearance she was asking for help all the while praying Jessup would find her—soon.

JESSUP

JESSUP AND JJ rode through the outer edges of town where they would not cause any suspicions with the trio. They reached the wooded area near the waterfront before Bill, Tom, and Liv. Quickly, they dismounted ready for action.

"Stay here, Jessup. Don't ask, do as I tell you. I'll be right back. I need you to trust me." JJ disappeared in the darkness before Jessup could say a word. He was back before he had decided it was time to go look for him.

"Jessup, listen. When Liv gets here, we gotta wait and be patient. We have to let her board the boat."

"Oh, hell no. We need to get to her before. There ain't no way she is getting aboard that boat. What are you thinking?"

"Please trust me." Something in his voice struck notes in Jessup's heart. Jessup knew JJ would never do anything to jeopardize Livvy's safety.

"JJ, you haven't ever steered me wrong. Ok, what do I need to do?"

"We wait until they board, and then we show up."

JJ

"ENTER." THE DEEP voice came in response to JJ's knock.

"Well look what the cat's drug in, Captain Jeremiah Johnson, himself. How are you doing, JJ?" Captain Martin grinned from ear to ear at the sight of his friend.

Quickly, JJ told Captain Martin what had happened to his sister-in-law and the interactions Jessup had with Bill and Tom.

"Bill is rough, but Tom, he is one to fear. I once saw him pick up a man by the head and flip him across the room. By the head."

Captain Martin let JJ know Bill had passed Liv off as a saloon girl who was willingly coming on the voyage but didn't want her husband, who was running the saloon, to know she was leaving him. "Aw, JJ, I am so sorry. When I saw her, I knew she was not a saloon girl."

He paused for a second. "I know you well enough," he said with a twinkle in his eye, "So what's the plan, and what do you need me to do?"

JJ and Jessup watched from the edge of the woods as Bill, Tom, and Liv dismounted and made their way up the ramp to board the boat. It was all Jessup could do to keep from running up and down the planks with guns blazing. "Wait a little longer," JJ said quietly to him as they watched from the treeline.

CAPTAIN MARTIN

CAPTAIN MARTIN WAS ready to receive his company when he heard a knock at his quarters.

"Enter."

"Captain, your riders have shown up, and they have a woman with them.

"Is the crew in place?"

"Yes, sir, everything is ready."

"Good. Let's go. Don't forget the signal."

"We are ready."

"So, you are here with the girl. Guess it concludes our deal, doesn't it Bill?"

"Looks like it, Captain Martin. Except for one more thing." Bill grinned. "I been thinking, she is worth more than a three-hundred-dollar gambling debt. I say you should throw in an extra two hundred dollars in cash and cancel the debt. This would make us square." Even Tom's eyes widened slightly.

"Well, boys, is she worth it?" Martin asked his crew.

The boat erupted in chaos. Martin grabbed Livvy, moving her out of the way as his crew descended on Tom and Bill. In the midst of the struggle, the pair finally gave up knowing it was futile to keep fighting.

Liv was confused and worried. Did she get exchanged from one set of problems for another?

"Missus Johnson, if you will do me the honor of escorting you aside, my men will take care of these swamp rats," Captain Martin said, giving her a smile.

Before she could answer, Jessup and JJ ran up the plank. Liv could no longer hold her tears as Jessup held her tightly.

JJ said, "Jessup and Liv, may I present to you my good friend who saved my life during one of our raids, Captain Mac Martin."

"We can't thank you enough for catching these two," Jessup replied. "Guess we need to get the marshal involved to put these guys in jail. Or hanging is always an option."

Captain Martin spoke up. "I have an idea, if I may. You know in our line of work we come across all types of ships needing labor crews and sometimes those new crew members only see topside and daylight when they shove their cold dead bodies as an offering to the sea many, many years later."

"You don't mean shanghai, do you?" Jessup asked. Liv looked confused.

The captain said, "What better revenge for kidnappers than to be 'kidnapped' themselves?" Tom and Bill both looked panic stricken.

Liv spoke up. "I see the same fear in their faces as I felt on my own. Sounds like the perfect plan to me."

"Liv, I need you to step over, out of the way," Jessup said as he pulled his gun from his holster.

"Now, you don't need to be doin' anything dumb...."

"I owe him this at least." Jessup grinned. He moved his finger from the trigger and grasped the gun by the cylinder allowing him to give Tom a hard rap on the head with the butt of the gun.

"All settled then? Hanson, take these two below and bind them well."

"Aye-aye, Captain Martin."

—Dr. Rebecca Foster was born in Wichita Falls, Texas during a tornado. This wild introduction into the world has taught her to be a calm force while the storms of life blow.

She and her husband, John, live in Austin, AR. They have enjoyed over 43 years as man and wife. He, she describes, is the love of her life and always her hero. They have three married daughters, seven grandsons, and one granddaughter.

In 2015, she earned her Doctorate Degree in Educational Leadership from Arkansas State University in Jonesboro. With over 25 years of experience in the field of education, she finally retired in May 2024. Her goals are to spend time with her husband, her writing and go back to school as a student.

Published work include contributions to Vault of Terror: Tales to Tell, Volume 1, Volume 2, Volume 5, Volume 7 *and the* White County Creative Writers Anthology 2018. *She is a member of the White County Creative Writers and enjoys listening and learning from the others in the group.*

Pretty Mother of the Night by Frederic Remington

LOST IN YOUR EYES

DIANA PARILLA

THE DOGS HEARD her first. That's how it always starts when you can't see what's coming. The dogs know before you do, and they tell you in their way. Mine quit their lazy panting and went still as stones. Then came the sound of hooves on hard ground, firm and sure, not like some drifter feeling their way through land that ain't theirs.

I set down the bucket I'd been carrying to the well and listened. Spring of '87, dry as old bones. One of those seasons where a man'll take company where he can get it, even if it comes with a side of trouble.

"Hello the house," came a voice. A woman's voice, which surprised me some. Distinct and strong.

"I'm here," I called back. "Come on up, if you're friendly."

She rode close enough that I could hear her horse breathing, hear the leather of her saddle creak when she shifted. The mare—I could tell by the sound—wasn't lathered up like she'd been ridden hard. Wasn't blowing or stamping neither.

That told me something about the woman before she ever spoke another word.

"Name's Naomi," she said. "Come from up Helena way. Heard there's fever down in Dillon, thought I'd wait it out somewhere quiet."

"This is quiet enough," I said. "Maybe too quiet for some folks."

She was quiet for a long moment. I heard her looking around, though I couldn't say how I knew that. You learn to hear things differently when you can't see them. The way someone shifts their weight tells you they're studying on something. The way they breathe tells you if they're nervous or calm or sizing you up for trouble.

"You live alone out here?" she asked.

"Just me and the dogs. Lost my sight some years back. Don't need much, and most folks don't need me." I gestured toward the lean-to built against the side of the house. "You're welcome to that shelter if you want it. Won't cost you nothing."

"That's kind of you." Her voice had changed. Softer, but careful too. "I got my own provisions. Won't be a burden."

That's how she came to be staying in my lean-to. She unsaddled her mare and turned her into my little corral with my two horses, and I heard her moving around. She didn't make unnecessary noise, which I appreciated. Most folks, when they're around someone who can't see, they talk too loud like you're deaf, too. She just moved natural, like my blindness was something she'd taken into account but didn't need to make a fuss over.

That night I cooked up beans and salt pork for two. She didn't say much while she ate, but when she finally spoke, something about it sat sideways with me. Had the sound of someone who'd been around books, or folks who had, not the sort that lived out of a saddlebag, bedded down under stranger's roofs, and rode out fevers with nobody but their horse for company.

"You said you lost your sight," she said when we were finished eating.

"Fire," I said, which was true enough as far as it went. "Few years back. House caught flame, and I got caught in it."

"Must've been hard, learning to live different."

"Still learning."

There was a fire, like I told her, but that wasn't the half of it. My brother Elijah was here then—younger than me, but full of big ideas about this country and what it might become. He had papers on this land, or said he did, and plans about railroad routes and mineral rights and Lord knows what else.

We fought that night. Fought about him selling the land out from under me, about forged boundary markers I'd found in his saddlebags, about promises he'd made to men I wouldn't trust to water my horses. The fight moved to the barn, and somewhere in the pushing and shoving, a lantern got knocked over. Last thing I remember clear was the smell of hay catching fire and the sound of Elijah yelling my name. Then a timber beam caught me across the head, and I went down in the smoke.

When I woke up a few days later, the barn was ash and my eyes were ruined and Elijah was gone. No sign of him anywhere, like he'd never been here at all. Sometimes I wondered if I'd killed him in that fire. Sometimes I hoped I had.

But I didn't tell Naomi none of that. Some things you keep buried, especially when you're not sure yourself what the truth of them is.

She asked a few more questions, like she was trying to map out who I was without seeming too interested. Where I'd come from originally, how long I'd been on this land, whether I had family anywhere. I answered what seemed safe to answer and kept the rest to myself.

That first night I woke to something touching my hair. Light as breath, fingers maybe, moving soft across the back of my neck. Made my skin prickle up and my heart start beating hard. But when I came full awake, one of the dogs was pressed against me, warm and solid. Could've been his fur I felt, or his nose snuffling at my head. Could've been her fingers, testing how deep I slept. Could've been my imagination, hungry for human touch after years of nothing but dog fur and my own rough hands.

In the morning, she was up before me and had coffee going. I heard her talking low to the horses, and her boots on the hard ground near the fence line that runs along the east side of my claim.

"Sleep all right?" she asked when I came out.

"Well enough. You?"

"I'm not much for sleeping easy in new places."

That was another thing that struck me odd. If she was from Helena like she said, traveling south to wait out fever, she should've been used to sleeping rough. Should've been the kind of woman who could curl up anywhere and get her rest. But she talked like someone who was particular about where she laid her head, like someone used to having her own place with her own bed and her own way of doing things.

The days fell into a rhythm after that. She'd be up early, tending her horse, then walking the fence line. Always had that rifle on her—I never saw it, but I didn't need to. I heard the strap shift when she moved, the click of the safety, the scrape of metal when she rested it against the post out front. You spend enough time blind, you start knowing things by sound and habit. And she made sure that rifle was always within arm's reach. I asked her about it once. She said a woman traveling alone couldn't be too careful. Said it like she'd had to learn that the hard way.

"What kind of trouble you expecting?" I asked.

"The kind that comes when you're not expecting it."

She had a way of saying things that sounded like answers but weren't. Like she was talking around something instead of about it. I was starting to think maybe she was running from something, or someone. Maybe that fever story was just something she told folks to explain why she wasn't where she was supposed to be.

About a week after she arrived, I was drawing water when I heard riders. Two of them, maybe three, moving along the ridge that looks down on my place.

I called to Naomi but she was already there beside me.

"Who is it?" I asked.

"Can't tell from here. Just men on horses."

"They looking this way?"

"Hard to say." She didn't say nothing right off. I could hear her jaw set, breath catch. "Probably just trappers passing through."

But her voice had gone tight, and I heard her shift her rifle from one hand to the other. Whatever she saw up on that ridge, it wasn't just trappers.

The riders moved on after a while, and we didn't see them again that day. But that night I smelled blood on her shirt when she sat down beside me after supper. Sharp and metallic, not like anything you'd get from gutting a rabbit or cleaning fish. This was different. Fresher.

"Cut yourself?" I asked.

"Caught my sleeve on barbed wire walking the fence. Nothing serious."

I didn't say anything to that, but I wondered. We didn't have much barbed wire, and what we had wasn't near where she'd been walking that evening. Besides, barbed wire cuts cloth, but it don't usually draw that much blood unless you really tangle with it.

It was maybe three days later, I heard the hammering. Heavy, regular sounds coming from the direction of the fence line. Someone driving posts, by the sound of it, or maybe stretching new wire. When I asked Naomi about it, she said she hadn't heard nothing.

"Someone's putting up new posts," I said.

"Why would someone do that?"

"Don't know. But that's what it sounds like."

She shut down then, the way she did when something I said made her think harder than she wanted to. I was starting to recognize that silence. It meant I'd touched on something she didn't want to talk about.

That evening she was quieter than usual. We sat outside listening to the night sounds—coyotes starting up somewhere to the west, my horses moving around in the corral, the wind picking up and rattling what was left of last year's grass. After a while she said, "Your fence don't stretch as far as you think."

"What do you mean?"

"Nothing. Just something I heard once."

We started talking then, really talking, like we'd known each other for years instead of days. She knew things about this country that surprised me—about the way land claims worked, about railroad routes and water rights, about which ranchers were buying up sections and which ones were selling out.

"You ever hear of a man named Elijah Reyes?" she asked, casual-like, after we'd been talking for a while.

My blood went cold. Nobody had spoken that name around me for years. "Might have. Why?"

"Just a name I heard mentioned down in town. Said he had a claim out this way somewhere."

"Don't know nothing about that," I said, but my voice hitched, traitor that it was.

She let it go, but I knew she was watching me in the dark. Not with her eyes—I couldn't see them anyway—but like she was trying to read something in the way I breathed, or the way I held my shoulders, or the way my voice had gone funny when she mentioned Elijah's name.

That night I lay awake a long while, listening to her stir around the lean-to. Heard her rise once, slip out toward the fence line, soft as a shadow. Came back about an hour later. I played dead asleep, but I don't reckon I fooled her much.

The fire started on a night when the wind was blowing hard from the west. I was sitting outside after supper when I caught the smell first—not smoke, but pitch. Bitter and resinous, like someone had been boiling pine sap. Then came the smoke, riding the wind down from the ridge.

"Naomi!" I called, but she didn't answer.

I got up fast, maybe too fast, and nearly stumbled over one of the dogs. The wind was picking up, and I could hear the fire now, crackling somewhere up where the bluff rises above the north end of my claim. That's where the old boundary markers were, the ones Elijah had set before... before everything went wrong.

I shuffled toward the corral, thinking I needed to get the horses ready in case we had to run. But when I got there, the fence rails were down and the corral was empty. All three horses gone, including Naomi's mare. That scared me worse than the fire. Animals know when to run, but they don't usually run before the danger gets close. Someone had turned them loose. Someone who knew what was coming.

The wind shifted, and the smoke rolled in thick. I made it to the well, hoping to draw some water—maybe soak the house, buy us a few more minutes. But when the bucket hit the bottom, it landed with a hollow thunk. Dry as dust. The well that never let me down, not even in the worst drought, was gone dry

That's when the dogs started barking. Not the usual bark for strangers or coyotes, this one was clipped and urgent, like they were trying to warn me about something real. I followed the sound, tripping over ground I thought I knew, coughing on smoke that tore at my throat and stung my busted eyes.

The barking snapped off right in the middle of a howl.

I shouted for Naomi one more time, but the wind took my voice and scattered it. Smoke choked the air, crawling closer with the fire. No longer just crackling—some beast, ravenous, roaring.

Then I heard something else. A gunshot cutting through the noise of wind and fire. Then another. Then silence.

I tried to get back to the house but lost my bearings in the smoke. Kept running into things that shouldn't've been there, tripping over rocks and ditches I didn't recall. My lungs were burning and my head was getting light. I sat down hard, thinking I'd rest just a minute, get my bearings, then figure out which way to go.

That's the last thing I remember clear for a while.

I woke up days later—three, maybe four, judging by the stubble on my face and the hollow ache in my belly. The air still smelled of smoke, but it was old smoke now, cold and settled. I was in my bed, and there was water beside it in a pitcher I didn't recognize, and some kind of stew in a bowl that was still warm enough to eat.

"Naomi?" I tried her name again, but I already knew she was gone. The silence felt different. Empty in a way it hadn't been since she arrived. A void filled only by its own vastness.

I slunk outside, dragging my steps like rusted chains. The house still stood, which caught me off guard. I traced scorch marks on the walls with my hands, and the porch roof had taken some fire, but the frame held firm. The lean-to was gone, though, burned away clean. Nothing left but the stone foundation and some warped metal from her saddle fittings.

But there were things in the house that hadn't been there before—sacks of flour and beans stacked neat in the corner, jerked meat wrapped in cloth, coffee and salt and sugar. Enough supplies to last weeks, maybe months, if I was careful with them.

The fence was gone too. I walked the whole line, or tried to, feeling with my feet for the post holes, the wire, anything that might tell me where my property ended and the rest of the world began. But there was nothing. Nothing but bare earth, and the acrid scent of scorched timber and melted steel.

It was near what used to be the northeast corner that I found her saddle blanket. Tucked under a rock so the wind wouldn't take it. When I picked it up, I felt something embroidered on one corner—letters, by the feel of them, though I couldn't make out what they said. E and R, maybe. Could've been anything.

There was something wrapped inside the blanket—a letter, by the weight and shape of it. Paper folded tidy and smooth. Quality stock, like what lawyers and land office men use for important documents.

I sat there for a long time holding that letter, running my fingers over it, trying to feel the words through the paper. My fingers had gotten good at reading surfaces, textures, the shape of things. But paper doesn't give up its secrets that way. The words stayed locked away from me, might as well have been written in a language I'd never heard.

For the first time since I lost my sight, that felt like a real loss. Not just an inconvenience or something I'd learned to work around, but a door slammed shut that I couldn't find the handle for.

About two weeks later, I heard another rider coming up the draw. This one announced himself proper before he got close, which told me he was either honest or smart about approaching a man who might be jumpy.

"Deputy Marshal Thomas," he called when he was still a ways off. "Mind if I water my horse?"

"Come ahead," I said. "Well's running again."

He was a talker, which was fine by me. I'd been alone long enough that even official conversation sounded good. Said he was riding through checking on folks after the fires, making sure everyone was all right.

"Hear you had some trouble up this way," he said while his horse drank.

"Some. Lost my fence and outbuildings. House made it through all right."

"Lucky thing. A lot of folks weren't so fortunate." He paused. "Land office was taking an interest in this section, what with the mineral rights and such. But they withdrew their claim last week. Said the fire damage made it not worth the legal trouble."

That stopped me cold. "Someone was contesting my claim?"

"Paperwork said so. Something about disputed boundaries and irregular filings. But it's all settled now. Fire burned out the coal seam up on the bluff, and without that, nobody wants to mess with the legal tangle. You're clear and legal, no question about it."

After he left, I sat thinking about what he'd said. About disputed boundaries and mineral rights I'd never heard of. About Naomi's questions, and her words—honed to some razor-thin perfection-way of talking that grated in a place like this. About her knowing the country better than she should have, and the blood on her shirt, and the gunshots I'd heard the night of the fire.

About Elijah.

I'd never told anyone the whole truth about what happened to my brother. Hell, I wasn't sure I knew it myself. But sitting there with that letter in my pocket, smoke still clinging to everything, pieces started fitting together in ways I didn't much like.

Elijah had been mixed up in something. The forged boundary markers I'd found, the talk about mineral rights, the men who came around asking questions after he disappeared. Maybe he'd sold claims he didn't have, or promised things he couldn't deliver. Maybe someone had come looking for him, and when they found me instead, they'd decided to wait and see what I knew.

Maybe Naomi hadn't been running from trouble. Maybe she'd been part of it.

The letter stayed folded in my worn jean pocket. Sometimes at night I'd take it out and try again to read it with my fingers, tracing the lines and curves of words I couldn't understand.

Summer ground on. I adjusted to the solitude, but it was a harsher lesson now. After a taste of companionship, even Naomi's odd brand, turned the quietness into a crushing weight. My hands found work—a fresh lean-to, timber cleared, the well flowing again.

Naomi. I reckon she was never who she said she was. Might've been some slick agent from the land office, come sniffing around to see if I still had fight left, to decide if this patch of earth was worth their trouble.

I figured her knowing this land so well meant she'd studied every marker, memorized every ridge and creek from some map tucked away in a city office back east. When I found boundary posts gone or moved, I thought she was setting up to wrest the claim away, bit by bit, with no one looking.

And when she clammed up at the mention of Elijah—that was a trick, I told myself. A way to dig at my guilt, see if I was the man who'd done him harm. Any slip could've been used against me, clearing the way for them to snatch this land with its owner locked up.

She said she came from Helena once, a long way off, the land office's seat. Made sense, that she'd be sent out, file her report, and vanish like smoke blown out of sight.

She could've taken my roof right out from under me. Maybe she'd even shot others with a stake in this land. The fire would've lowered its value, made it easier for her or whoever she worked for.

I kept thinking about that saddle blanket she left behind. Smelled of juniper and sweat and wind. There were letters stitched near the hem—*E.R.,* if my fingers weren't fooling me. Could've stood for Elijah Reyes. Or maybe not.

Could be she came hunting revenge. To see who'd finished off her man. Or maybe she already knew what kind of man he was, and came to wipe his name off the map before it dragged her down too.

Some nights I wondered if Elijah came back to finish what he'd started—that fight that took my sight. Maybe he wasn't done with me. And maybe she wasn't his wife at all. Just someone passing through. Saw what he was, put an end to it. That'd explain the gunshots. The way she never told the full of anything. The way she had something of his.

The fire didn't take the house. It took the lines, the posts, the reasons men had to circle this land like buzzards. Left me breathing, barely, but breathing still.

Afterward, there were sacks of flour in the cellar that weren't there before. A fresh barrel of water, though the well had run dry. I didn't put them there.

She left the land to me. Walked away before I could ask her why. Maybe she saw I wasn't the man she feared I'd be. Or maybe she just needed to believe there was still one good man left standing. That's the story I told myself. That's the one I wanted to believe, even if it didn't line up with what she'd written in that letter.

I couldn't read no stories, so I had to scratch out my own, patched up from scraps and wild guesses, knowing the truth'd stay lost behind these blind eyes. Told myself little tales at night. My eyes were no good, but my head still worked.

One evening in late summer, I was sitting outside with my back against the rough wood when the dogs perked up again. Same way they had that first day, going from lazy and content to alert and listening in the space of a heartbeat. I heard boots hit hard dirt, steps that didn't waste time, like the person knew damn well where they were headed.

The door creaked open behind me.

"You're back," I said, not bothering to turn. I already knew—or maybe just wanted to believe it was who I hoped for.

"Yes." Her voice, clear as a bell. Like I could ever forget.

"Why?"

"To read you the letter."

"What letter?" I asked, my fingers tracing the edge of the folded paper tucked deep in my pants pocket. I kept it close, no way I'd risk it getting scorched or soaked without warning.

"Didn't you find it? Well, doesn't matter."

"Probably not."

"And? I'll answer all your questions. If you have any."

"Of course I do—more than one," I said, jerking around toward what to me sounded like a voice sent straight from heaven. "Beans and salted pork sound good for supper? You reckon the horses need a drink before then?"

—*Diana Parrilla, born in Spain, is a keen reader and passionate writer with diverse interests. With her degree in economics and mastery of Japanese, she is always eager to learn new things, especially languages, which she views as a way to open her eyes to new worlds that once felt unattainable, just like reading and writing. She shares her passion for anime and games on her YouTube channel through reviews, translations, and language learning tips. Her handle on social media is @buffyta17. She has published works across horror, romance, mystery, and speculative fiction. Her stories have appeared in Inkd Publishing's* Impulse Anthology, *West Avenue Publishing's* Secrets of the Snow Globe, *Dark Holme Publishing's* Dark Descent: Whispers from Beyond Vol.1, *and in various anthologies from Dragon Soul Press, Black Hare Press, Murderous Ink Press, Three Ravens Publishing, and more. She was awarded first prize in the Autumn 2024 Mollie Savage Memorial Science Fiction & Fantasy Writing Contest, hosted by* Toasted Cheese Literary Journal, *and earned an Honorable Mention in the* Writers of the Future *contest (2nd Quarter, 2025).*

HOPE NEVER DIES

DENISE F. McALLISTER

SARAH EMMA WAS always up before the rest of the family, preparing breakfast before the sun showed its face. From a young age, her mother had taught her how to avoid the wrath of her father—coffee and food. It was almost ready. Beans warming on the stove. Dried jerky meat. Kneading dough for the biscuits.

She was grateful for the arrival of cool spring days, a stark contrast to the harsh Michigan winters that brought painfully frigid trips to the hen house.

A rumbling sound nearly shook the wooden cabin. Snoring. Like the fierce wind from a blizzard bellowing through the rafters. The men in her family expected the females to handle the cooking and cleaning. If only they'd say a kind word once in a while or offer a little help. But they were downright lazy, letting fences fall and weeds grow to their knees.

Christine was a gentle woman with the Good Book always close by. She had named her sons Matthew, James, and Luke. The father, Gus, never displayed much enthusiasm for his children. "I brought you into this world, and I can take you out." Unforgiving, like the winters, there were no warm smiles to thaw out his icy personality.

Christine told Sarah Emma that Gus had been different in his younger years. Before the heartache his father had inflicted upon him with daily beatings, before alcohol.

Sarah Emma pounded the dough with a faraway stare. She recalled, when she was small, how her mother taught her how to make biscuits, and they laughed as the flour sifted over their heads, coating their hair. It was the last time Sarah felt carefree.

Her mother smiled. "Punch it like you're mad at someone."

Little Sarah Emma balled up her fists and gave the dough hard jabs. "You'll get the hang of it, Sweetie."

Father Gus stumbled to the table, but Sarah Emma still came to him. "Morning, Papa."

With outstretched arms, she reached for a hug. Her angelic face quickly turned to a frown at the foul breath emitting from his mouth, frozen in a giant yawn. Rubbing his eyes, he scratched his disheveled mop of hair as well as other body parts.

"Pooh, stinky Papa." The little girl hadn't learned yet about keeping her thoughts to herself.

Christine gently pulled Sarah Emma away.

"What did you say, little she-devil? How dare you talk to me like that."

He swiped at her but connected with his wife's thigh as she pushed Sarah behind her.

"Uh." She rubbed her leg. "Gus, she's just a child."

A diabolic expression fixed on his whisker-covered face. "Who's gonna clean up this mess?" The flour colored the floor and table. "And where the heck is my coffee? You're both useless."

"I'll get it right away. Breakfast is nearly ready."

When Christine turned to the stove to lift the coffee pot with a towel, her husband yanked Sarah Emma's skinny arm.

"You're not gettin' away just yet, you little witch. You deserve a whippin' and that's what I'm gonna give you."

Sarah screamed. "No, Papa. Please don't hurt me." He had before, lots of times.

He angrily hauled her over his lap and swatted her bottom with a merciless hand. One. Two. Three. Four.

Her mother told her not to cry. But Sarah Emma didn't know how to keep the water inside her little eyes. It seemed impossible no matter how hard she squeezed them tight. The tears started to flow.

Christine intervened. "Please, Gus, don't hurt her. She's too young to understand."

"Then get her out of my sight. Shoulda been a boy. Hurry up and pour my coffee, woman!"

The older sons snickered whenever Sarah or the youngest boy, Luke, got smacked. Anyone could see they were copying their father's personality. Their full-of-themselves nature often manifested into a curt, disrespectful word and attitude toward their mother and sister.

"It's a female's job to cook and clean," the oldest loudly said as he puffed out his chest. He whispered with the middle son about other things a woman was good for.

Sarah Emma learned it was best to steer clear of Matthew. There had been too many times when he pushed her down or kicked mud on her clean dress, threatening to beat her if she tattled. He called her "Useless Runt."

Only Luke showed kindness, which brought insults from the father. Gus repeatedly told him, "You can't be nice in this world. People will walk all over you. You're too much like your Ma."

Sarah Emma pounded the dough again to wake from her daydream. There were many sad childhood memories she wished she could block out—a home filled with anger, hitting, and crying. Christine was the peacemaker and said the Bible encouraged her to love our enemies and to be strong in the face of injustice. She frequently said, "Hope never dies."

Sarah wasn't so sure about that. She knew she could never be the angel on earth like her mother. A tear fell from her eye into the dough. Maybe it would sweeten the men in her family as they wolfed down the biscuits. But no tears contained magic properties. The men were just plain rotten. Except for Luke of course. He was her one friend. Sometimes he hid her when their father was on a rampage. And he always stepped in to take a beating in her place.

Although Sarah Emma's childhood seemed to be a never-ending

nightmare of sadness and abuse, she cherished memories of the times her father and brothers took horse scouting trips, leaving Christine, Luke, and Sarah at home.

In springtime, Gus and the older boys gathered wild horses and drove them to other towns for sale. Luke once whispered to Sarah that he had overheard them talking about where to find the horses. He suspected they were stolen.

Christine turned the week of the horse hunt into a time of fun and love. She let them sleep in longer than normal, until the aroma of sizzling bacon beckoned them awake.

"Children," her sweet voice sang. "Breakfast is ready. Come and get it."

"Coming, Mama."

"Get your brother up too, sweetheart."

Sarah Emma climbed the ladder and found Luke still snoozing. Tip-toeing, she'd wake him with their secret signal—lightly touching his sealed eyelashes until they fluttered open.

The trick was on her. Faking slumber, as soon as her finger touched his lash, his teenage hand grabbed her slender arm, but not rough.

"Gotcha!" he said with a big grin.

She squealed and headed for the ladder. "Luke, you scared me! Hurry down. Breakfast's ready."

His hands became like two bear claws. "I'm gonna get you." Playfully, his fingers stretched toward her long braids.

More squealing, but she was faster to slide down the ladder. Thank goodness she wore boy pants today instead of a dress, which helped her fly with ease. She preferred wearing denims like her brothers instead of frilly dresses. Luke wasn't too far behind, nearly leaping to the floor and bypassing all the rungs.

Their mother smiled as she set plates of scrambled eggs, jerky, and biscuits on the table. The small bouquet of wild flowers arranged in a stone pitcher added to the cheery display.

"You two are full of energy this morning. Settle down so your stomachs are not all a'jumble."

"We going hunting today, Mama?"

"Yes, sweetheart. I'm packing a picnic to take to the lake."

"Feels like it'll be warm enough for a swim."

Father and brothers would return in two days, so if they wanted some fun, it'd have to be today.

"Yes, dear. Hunting and swimming." Turning to Luke she asked, "Which guns will you bring?"

"The old Colt revolver. And the Spencer repeater. You never know when bears might be in the area waking up from their big nap. Or deer. We could sure use one."

"Good boy," Christine said. "You're a skilled hunter, maybe the best in the family. Let's give thanks, have breakfast, and do our chores so we can get to that sparkling lake."

Before they prayed, Sarah piped up. "I'm a good hunter too, Mama."

"Yes, you are, my brave girl." Christine looked at her teenage children. "Just don't let your father find out. He would not be happy with our outing. I'll take responsibility and repent to God for keeping the secret."

After breakfast, Luke readied the horse and wagon, and his mother and sister loaded supplies. As they ambled along a dirt trail, Christine sang. The kids were familiar with "Amazing Grace," but they were lost in the lyrics of "Old Aunt Sally" and "God Bless our Native Land." Mother never sang around Father anymore.

It was a beautiful day filled with laughter. Sarah and Luke had been swimming together since they were little when Christine had let them jump in wearing their "birthday suits." Not now though of course. Sarah was a young lady and would keep her underdress on. Luke wore his long underwear. Christine rolled her black stockings off and waded ankle deep, no further. It would not be becoming, she said.

She busied herself with the food preparation—pickled hard boiled eggs, cucumbers, hardtack crackers, beef jerky. And of course, for dessert, her famous "Apple Brown Betty"—a cobbler creation with lots of brown sugar and cinnamon.

After splashing Sarah mercilessly, Luke emerged from the cold lake and declared himself "starving" as he plopped down on a blanket.

His mother handed him a towel and shirt. "Be sure to dry off so you don't catch a chill."

Luke grinned and held his arms up to display his developing muscles just like the picture of the sideshow strong man he had seen in dime novels.

When Sarah joined them, the little band of kindred spirits settled into a comfortable peace. Sarah wished her entire family could be loving and care for one another. But, for whatever reason, she knew it was not to be.

"Mmm," Luke grunted. "This Brown Betty is so good, Mother. Thanks for making it."

"Of course, son. Anything for you and Sarah Emma."

"Anything?" he asked.

It was apparent the conversation was about to take a serious turn. Sarah's eyes darted from her brother to her mother.

"What's on your mind, Luke?"

"Sarah and I have discussed this. We know Father doesn't have much regard for me. The last time, he covered my body with welts and wounds, and nearly killed me. Remember? And he's given you more beatings than you care to admit."

It was true. All of it. Christine's eyes filled with tears.

"Mother, you know he's becoming more violent... with me, and with Sarah Emma. We cannot live like this."

Christine didn't say a word, just shook her head slightly back and forth.

Sarah Emma was determined to speak calmly. "Father wants me to marry Mister Schweegle. He made a deal with the old man. Mama, I won't do it."

"Might not be that bad." Christine barely looked at her daughter. "You are of marrying age. Mister Schweegle would take care of you."

Luke spoke firmly. "Mother, you know that man is mean. He's old and disgusting. He'll beat Sarah Emma like he did his first wife. And use her up... in an unmentionable way."

"I could talk to Father."

Luke shook his head. "It's too late for talking, Mother. I saw a flyer in town about recruits for the volunteer army. The war has been waging for a year now. They need men. I want to enlist. I'll find a place for Sarah... with church folks, to be sure. We want you to come too."

"If you go, Luke, I'll never see you again. Besides, it wouldn't be right in the eyes of God for me to leave my husband and your brothers."

"They're cruel like Father. We can't stay. The army will give me meals and lodging. The training is not too far from here. You can come visit."

"You could be killed, Luke. I don't want to lose you. Or Sarah Emma. It's no place for a young lady."

Luke grabbed his rifle and placed the revolver on the blanket.

"My mind is made up, Mother. I'm a man now." He nodded to his sister. "Sarah and I will try to find a deer. Keep this gun with you. Fire it if you need us."

As the two headed into the woods, Sarah saw her mother covering her eyes with her palms, tears flowing.

"Luke, maybe that was too harsh for Mama?"

He marched with determination, but slowed so as not to make a thunderous ruckus and scare off any game.

"It had to be said, Sarah. We can't live with Father. We must go. Terrible things could happen if we don't."

"I want to go. I'm not marrying that disgusting Mister Schweegle."

"Shh. Let's find our spot. I hear some rustling."

"I worry about leaving Mama. Father might hurt her."

Luke was quiet.

Sarah went on in a low tone. "You spoke about the army, Luke. I was thinking... I'm a real good shot. Maybe they'd take me on too, let me enlist."

"What? You're a fourteen-year-old girl. How could you join the army?"

"Mother and I read a book about a female pirate captain. She cut her hair and learned to take up the sword. She led a band of men."

"Oh, Sarah, life is not like the fables in a book." He abruptly put his hand over her mouth that was starting to open. "Shh... listen."

He took up the rifle, but she reached out to stop him. "Let me. You bagged the last one a few months ago."

"Okay, but go slow," he whispered.

They crouched behind a clump of bushes and Sarah carefully peered over them. She supported the rifle as Luke had taught her and squinted an eye. Certain she saw movement, she let her breath seep out.

"Slow and easy." Luke said quietly. "Now. Shoot."

She pointed the rifle and pulled the trigger.

It was far away. Shadowy. Camouflaged by bushes and rocks. Sarah thought she saw other deer, or something, emerging from the woods.

She was excited. "I got him!"

A big thud sounded, but was that a deer? Then an audible human sound. "Uhhh!" Horses scampered, hollers shrieked. A voice yelled, "Pa! You okay?"

What? Pa? Was that her brothers and father?

Immediately, everything felt wrong. She slowly started to stand for a better look. Chaotic images flashed before them.

"No, Sarah, get down." Luke yanked her into the brush, his eyes frantic. "Oh, dear Lord. It's Father." Luke's face was white in shock.

Sarah's speech came out clipped. "Father? He is not due back yet." Then she said the unimaginable words, "Is he dead?"

"I don't know, Sarah. We have to get out of here before they see us."

"What do you mean? We should help him."

"If he's wounded, we'll get a beating. If he's dead, Matthew and James will become heads of household, and they'll beat us, maybe even kill us. You know how they are. Let's make our way back to Mother. Duck in here, Sarah. Be quiet." Luke pulled her deeper into the bushes. They crouched together and made themselves small as they listened to the riders.

Luke and Sarah didn't hear much as the horses passed, but they saw their father, and they heard enough to put the fear of God into them.

"Is he breathing?" Matthew screamed at James who held the lead to their father's horse next to his. Gus was slumped but the boys had securely tied him to the saddle. Blood trailed from his side, down his leg, to the horse's flank.

Matthew barked again. "Make sure he stays upright. We got to get him to town. Doc will patch him up."

A gurgling sound came out of Gus's mouth along with a glob of blood. "Uh... who... who shot me?"

Matthew spoke evenly, trying to maintain some semblance of calm. "We don't know, Pa. We gotta get you to the doc."

They headed to the road in the opposite direction from where Christine had set up her picnic.

"Uh... where's your mother? And those other two good-for-nothin's." He coughed and held his side, blood drenching his pants.

"Probably home, Pa." Matthew's face displayed a myriad of emotions—shock and anger but also fear. "Hold on."

The father's head slumped again to his chest, but first he muttered, "I'll kill 'em. None of 'em are loyal. They've been lying to me. I know they do things when we're away...."

Luke and Sarah hardly took a breath, just stayed hidden in the bushes. But they heard his deadly threat.

Soon, they ran to the wagon where Christine was packing up the supplies.

She turned in their direction. "I heard the gunshot. Did you get a deer?"

Luke held her arms and stared into her eyes.

"Mother, something terrible has happened. We thought it was a deer and Sarah took her shot. They were covered by the bushes. It's Father and the boys. They came back early. Father was shot. It was an accident."

Sarah Emma burst into tears. "I'm so sorry, Mama. I didn't know it was him."

Christine was shocked, but she did not cry. She had experience with crises over the years, especially when her husband beat her. She had willed herself not to cry then, and wouldn't now.

"Should I go help him? Or... is he... uh... dead?"

Luke spoke. "We had to get out of there. You know what they'll do to us if they find out Sarah shot him. We heard him say he'd kill us."

Christine's eyes fixed on her son, only sixteen but already a man. "He's probably delirious, in shock. But he'll be angry, to be sure. Should I stay here and you take the horse off the wagon? Maybe hide for a while until he recovers?"

"No, that would be suspicious, you being out here with a wagon but no horse. Mother, we have to leave for good. Come with us."

They all had to think fast.

Finally, Christine spoke.

"Leave me here with the wagon and horse. Hide in the woods. I'll tell them you ran away earlier, and I came here to pray."

Luke asked, "What about the picnic food? They'll know we were with you."

"Leave me a little. Take the rest for your journey."

"We won't get far on foot, Mother," Luke said.

"Get to the O'Reilly farm. They always said they'd help me. They have two extra horses. Tell them we'll pay them back. I'm sure they'll do it. Swear them to secrecy."

Christine hugged her children tight and shed more tears.

"Please, Mama," Sarah pleaded. "Come with us. They'll hurt you."

"No." Christine stroked Sarah's hair. "They'll need me to cook and doctor Father's wound." She gave a little chuckle as if to say that's all she was good for.

Her face showed inner strength. "Luke, protect her. Don't write to me. Sarah Emma, cut your braids, wear a hat. Dress like a man, don't speak. Remember the pirate book we read. That woman was brave. You are too." She gave a tiny smile and hugged them again but quickly released.

"Oh, Mama."

"I'll be praying for you. Maybe God will let us meet again. Now, go. Hurry. And hide."

Luke kissed his mother's cheek and said, "We'll come back for you one day. I promise."

Sarah was conflicted. In her young life, she had always helped those in pain. Her father was bleeding, but she did nothing. She was the one to cause all this heartbreak.

But she knew her father and older brothers were capable of evil. She dreamed of a new, good life. That would mean running to freedom. Luke was right about everything. They'd have to leave their mother and run and hide from their father. If he was still alive.

Luke and Sarah ran like their lives depended on it, which of course they did. Sarah had never felt such fear. She was sure her father and older brothers might jump out from around the bend and hurt her and Luke. And then go back for their mother.

She had to be strong. She forced herself to breathe and remember some of her mother's sayings.

Don't cry. You can do it. Just like the woman pirate. Hope never dies.

The O'Reillys kindly gave them two horses, and Luke and Sarah vowed to pay them back. Mr. O'Reilly would tell their father that he had never seen them. It was obvious he had little respect for Gus.

After running the horses hard, away from town and well-known trails, Sarah and Luke stopped. It was nearly dark and they could all use a break—horses and humans.

Sarah wanted to keep going, even ride through the night in case her older brothers were on their tail. But she agreed to a brief rest.

"Maybe they're taking care of Father and not even following us," Luke said.

She shook her head. "He probably ordered them to find us rather than being nursemaids."

Luke tied his horse to a sturdy branch near an outcropping of rocks. He cleared his throat. "Sarah, if, for some reason, they find our trail and if they... uh... if they capture me... I want you to ride as fast as you can. Anywhere. Hide and don't look back. I'll get away somehow. Don't worry about me."

She could tell this was hurting him, but he was older and always had protective feelings for her. He had to say this. It was his job as a man, although she wasn't exactly sure where he learned it since their father was so awful.

She stared intensely into his eyes. It was as though she was gaining every ounce of courage in her small body... from somewhere... and growing up years before her time.

"I'll never leave you, Luke. You're my family. You and Mama."

Reaching into her bag, she retrieved a knife and started chopping on one of her long braids.

"What are you doing?" Luke started to grab her hand.

"No, stop. I've got to do this. I will do this. I don't ever want to be caught and sent back to Papa. I'll join the army if I can. I'm not a little girl anymore."

Luke grabbed her shoulders. His eyes glistened like a dark, foreboding river. "I'm sorry, Sarah. Wish it was different. But you're strong. You're going to do great things with your life."

"I just want us to be free."

"Let me help." Luke took the knife and sawed on her braid. He had always said her rich, auburn-colored hair matched their mother's. Sarah could see this was torturing him.

She gathered her bag, including her braids which she'd discard elsewhere so no one would find them.

Luke rubbed dirt between his palms, then applied some to her sweet face around the jawline. "Here, maybe you'll look more like a boy."

Her chest filled with a deep breath, her shoulders squared, and her lips pressed together. The sun wasn't even up yet.

"Let's ride," Sarah Emma said. "We've got places to go. And lives to live. Good, free lives. Remember, hope never dies."

Luke saluted her. "Yes, sir. Lead on."

AUTHOR'S NOTE

This story started with a seed of an idea loosely based on the real life of Sarah Emma Edmonds (1841-1898). In 1857, she left rural New Brunswick, Canada to escape her abusive father and an arranged marriage and ended up in Michigan. When war was declared in 1861, Edmonds enlisted in the Union army disguised as a man. In 1865, she published a memoir of her adventures in which she claimed to have been a spy for the Union army.

—*Denise F. McAllister first wrote stories when she was about ten years old. After entering the working world, her life was submerged into corporate jobs. Even though those positions often made use of her writing, editing, and communication skills, she never forgot her first love of creative writing. Since 2015, she has been making time for those pursuits. McAllister has co-authored nine Contemporary Western novels (Wild Cow Ranch and Rafter O Ranch) about a strong, young woman on a Texas ranch. Recently she authored a three-book series (The Katy McKim Mysteries) about a woman who discovers criminal acts at horse shows. When not writing, she is busy editing other authors' projects. A member of Western Writers of America, Women Writing the West, the Booth Western Art Museum's writers guild, as well as other organizations, McAllister advises writers to get connected and never stop learning. While in awe of Western terrain, she is also grateful to live in the verdant landscape of Georgia.*

Arapahos by Alfred Jacob Miller

COMANCHE MOON

R.K. OLSON

"SERGEANT, YOU WILL attend the post dance. That's an order," said
U.S. Army Captain Hind.

"Yes, sir!"

Hind leaned back in his chair and observed the barrel-chested soldier
with a sun-blasted face, standing gun-barrel straight. The soldier's short,
dark hair bristled on his head and crow's feet sprouted at the corners
of his eyes. Army records said they were both thirty-years old and an
inch under six-feet-tall with a decade of service each in the U.S. Army.

Hind placed the palms of his slender hands flat on the desk and his
voice softened. "I mentioned your bravery in the official report docu-
menting the defense of Brown's ranch from the Comanche. The report
and commendation for bravery are part of your permanent record."

"Thank you, sir!"

Hind paused. The air in the windowless office was thick. He caught
snatches of the bustle of men and horses outside on the Camp Verde
parade ground.

Sergeant Matthews remained at attention. His brown eyes stared
at a spot behind Captain Hind on the wall, a few inches over his head.

"Congratulations," said Hind, standing up. "You are being promoted to first sergeant. Pay is retroactive to four months ago. Well deserved. Army headquarters got something right, for a change."

"Thank you, sir," said Sergeant Matthews, snapping a salute. Hind returned the salute.

"I am announcing your promotion at the post dance. That's why you need to be there."

"I'll be there in dress uniform, sir." Matthews set his meaty shoulders back another inch. His eyes flickered for an instant across the captain's clean-shaven face.

"Very good. Well deserved." Hind's chair creaked when he sat back down. "Your enlistment is coming up soon. The Army values your Comanche fighting experience. I encourage you to re-enlist."

"Thank you, sir. The Army has been good to me," said Matthews, eyes fixed back on the wall over Hind's head.

"The Army is a cold mistress, but at least you don't have in-laws to deal with."

The captain moved in his chair, generating another protesting creak.

"I want you to keep an eye on the new lieutenant. Stanton doesn't know what he doesn't know. Dismissed."

Matthews saluted, spun on his heel, and marched out the door.

———————⋙⟐⋘———————

FIRST SERGEANT MICHAEL Matthews stepped out into the glare of the slanting late afternoon sun with a grin on his rugged face.

First sergeant pays thirty dollars a month. That's one hundred and twenty dollars back pay! I could buy some land. I'm the highest ranking NCO in the camp.

He placed his worn, dusty brown, wide-brimmed slouch hat on his head and pulled the brim low over his eyes. Camp Verde's parade ground was empty and baked in the Texas sun. A blazing yellow sun looked pasted onto a canvas of bright blue.

He breathed in, expanding his chest and bracing his legs. The sergeant's pants were sky blue with a yellow calvary stripe down the side of each leg. The sun had faded his dark blue flannel shirt with three chevrons displayed on the sleeve. He'd sew on the extra insignia, a small diamond signifying he was now a first sergeant, before the post dance.

He crossed his arms over his chest and pressed his lips together, losing the grin.

Re-enlist? Ten years passed already? It feels like just yesterday it was 1846, and I was twenty-years old, all full of piss and vinegar.

He'd enlisted for the chance to see Texas, and he'd found a home in the Army.

He squinted and scanned Camp Verde with its collection of stone and wooden buildings serving as barracks, storage, and stables stretched out along the San Antonio-El Paso Road. Beyond the dusty road was rocky, dry Texas Hill Country with rugged limestone hills dotted with mesquite and cedar, sometimes oak.

His face contorted as a breeze carried the stink of camels to his nose. The Army was testing camels as pack animals in the southwest. Camp Verde housed fifty camels corralled in a one hundred and fifty foot long and ten foot high stone wall enclosure.

The camels were smelly, filthy animals with nasty dispositions. The North African handlers that came with the camels weren't much better.

Without warning, the camel pen's gate flew open and two soldiers staggered out at a stumbling run. Matthews watched an angry spitting camel bare its teeth and trumpet a deep, guttural roar chasing the soldiers. A dark-skinned shirtless man in red pants shouted in a foreign language and waved a goading stick in his hand. The camel stamped its feet and whipped its head up and down and side-to-side.

The horse stables nearby exploded with snorts and high-pitched squeals as the still unfamiliar, rank camel stench and vocalizations frightened and panicked the horses.

A second camel handler lassoed the camel's front legs with a roping pole. The red-panted handler avoided a bone snapping kick and dropped a rope around the shrieking camel's neck. Wheezing and chest heaving, the animal tired out. A handler wedged a wooden nose peg into the camel's nostrils. The second handler covered the camel's head with a calming wet burlap sack.

"Wilcox! Jennings! Get over here on the double!" shouted Matthews at the two soldiers. His voice was as rough as tree bark.

The two soldiers came to attention in front of the sergeant. Matthews stared down at the two lean, shorter men, hands clasped behind his back. A camel handler shook his fist at the soldiers and said something unintelligible. He led the camel back into the corral.

The sergeant cleared his dry throat. "What the hell were you doing?"

Standing ramrod straight, arms by his side and thumbs on the yellow stripe on the seams of his trousers, red-haired Jennings said, "Corporal Bernard ordered us to help with the camels."

Matthews declared, hands on hips, "You layabouts are not fit for camel wrangling. You're reassigned to latrine duty. I'll inspect the latrines before dinner. Dismissed!"

Just then, Matthews heard iron-rimmed wagon wheels grinding across the dirt parade ground. The wagons were twelve-foot long prairie schooners with white canvas coverings stretched over wooden bows. They were followed by ten mounted troopers whose dark blue shirts were dusty, with white sweat stains caked down the back. Sweat glistened on their horses' flanks.

Four mules pulled each wagon. One prairie schooner turned out to be an Army surveying team. The other was a civilian heading out to claim a patch of Texas for himself.

Matthews walked toward the wagon and spied Lieutenant Stanton pushing his long, straight blond hair back over his ears and smoothing his Van Dyke mustache. Stanton marched across the parade ground bringing his trim figure to attention next to Captain Hind and the cavalry officer that arrived with the troopers.

Matthews was inspecting the wagon axles when he looked up into a beautiful olive-skinned face framed by raven black hair tumbling to her shoulders. The large, dark eyes melted the sergeant into his boots. She was slim, shapely, and smiling.

The petite woman grasped his hand to step down. She placed one foot onto a stool provided for that purpose and then hopped to the ground. She slowly lifted her head, looking at him with lips slightly parted. Her head reached the height of Matthews' shoulders. He fumbled, removing his campaign hat. She smoothed out the long skirt and tailored jacket of her matching brown riding habit.

Inclining her head toward the sergeant, she said, "I'm Lena Randolph." Her smile flashed strong white teeth contrasting with her sun-bronzed skin.

"Sergeant Matthews, at your service, ma'am."

"Thank you, sir." Lena reached into a pocket and pulled out a crisp, white sun bonnet. She put it over her dark hair and tied it under her chin.

His face flushed as his brain raced to come up with something to say.

"The sun can be wicked in Texas, ma'am."

"Yes indeed, Sergeant."

"Sergeant Matthews!" shouted Lieutenant Stanton, striding across the parade ground. "See to the wagons."

Then, with a bow and a flourish, doffing his Hardee hat like a medieval knight errant, Lieutenant Stanton said to Lena, "Allow me to introduce myself. I am Lieutenant Gerald Stanton. The captain has requested I escort you to his office."

"We shouldn't keep the captain waiting," replied Lena. They crossed the parade ground side-by-side. Matthews could hear her merry laugh at a quip offered by the lieutenant.

He looked away, realizing he'd been staring after her.

That night, in the darkness of his bunk, he could see Lena Randolph smiling at him, her eyes sparkling. Matthews walked outside in his long johns with his tobacco pouch. He tilted his head up and gazed at the moon.

We'll get a Comanche Moon soon.

It was called a Comanche Moon because its brightness allowed for swift, stealthy travel across vast terrain, making it ideal for nighttime raids. He blew long streams of tobacco smoke at the moon as the purple morning light washed over the landscape.

Promotion to First Sergeant is as high as I'll get.

Army life was boredom, dust, and drills with Comanche attacks providing brief moments of sheer terror. He had no regrets about his chosen path. However, Lena Randolph sparked something lying dormant. It excited him and kept him on edge at the same time. One moment excited by the future and the next afraid to give up what he had.

Corporal Bernard said he'd heard that Lena was a Mexican and Comanche mix. Bernard said that's two strikes against her and a fancy education doesn't mean she wouldn't scalp you in your sleep.

"STANTON, I WANT you and the sergeant with ten troopers to escort the surveying wagon with Lieutenant and U.S. Army Surveyor Hancock, a civilian surveyor, and Miss Randolph to Fort Lancaster. Sergeant you're responsible for provisioning. You'll use six camels for carrying food, ammunition, and equipment."

Matthews and Stanton were at attention, but Stanton's face sagged with the effects of liquor.

"I want the wagon and camels ready to go at first light tomorrow. And Sergeant, I'll see you at the post dance tonight. Stanton, get some breakfast. Dismissed."

Both men saluted and tramped out of the office.

"Any orders, sir?" asked Matthews outside the captain's office.

Stanton massaged his temple with his fingers. Then, with a brittle edge to his voice, he said, "You have your orders, Sergeant." Stanton paused, adding, "I heard the Randolph woman is part Comanche squaw. Good looking, but you can't trust her." He strode off, leaving Matthews tight lipped and brow creased.

The sergeant caught glimpses of Lena during the day while he gathered supplies. The gossips said she was Old Man Randolph's youngest daughter, a teacher and had a full-blooded Comanche grandmother.

The handful of women at Camp Verde gave Lena hard, stiff smiles. Many had friends and relatives killed by the Comanche. They neglected organizing the usual welcoming tea for new female arrivals. A wag in the barracks said Lena would do a war dance at the post dance that evening.

SERGEANT MATTHEWS SHRUGGED into his dark blue frock coat with brass buttons and yellow piping. He polished his black brogan's and brushed his Hardee hat.

Glowing lantern light transformed the supply building across the parade ground into the site for tonight's dance. To his ear, the laughter and music mixed to create a joyful sound, full of expectations.

Their eyes met as soon as he entered the building. The fiddle band was in the far corner of the room, taking a break to mop their faces. The air in the room was hot and sticky. Boxes, chairs, and tables lined the walls to make room for dancing. Paper flower decorations hung from the ceiling. The punch bowl ladle was getting a workout.

"Good evening, Sergeant Matthews," said Lena. "I understand Lieutenant Stanton is in charge of sentry duty and will be busy until midnight."

"Yes, ma'am," replied Matthews.

"Please, call me Lena."

"Michael."

"May I have your attention please!" said Captain Hind. "Sergeant Matthews, front and center."

Curious looks cascaded across faces of two dozen guests as the captain read an excerpt from his report, lauding the actions of Sergeant Matthews in defending the Brown family's ranch from a Comanche raid. The sergeant stood at attention next to the captain, his brass buttons reflecting the lantern light.

"It is my distinct pleasure to be the first to salute First Sergeant Michael Matthews!" added the captain, sounding like a circus ringmaster.

The sergeant and Lena danced every dance. During the fiddle band breaks, they strolled outside for cool fresh air and conversation. He ignored the sidelong glances and tight-lipped looks cast in Lena's direction.

Lena shared that her grandfather had arrived in Texas years ago when it was mesquite, rocks, and Indians. He married a Comanche and carved out a ranch that his son, Lena's father, ran today. Her father sent Lena back east for an education. She returned as a teacher and was starting a school in El Paso.

"I am a Randolph with a Mexican mother and Comanche blood in my veins," said Lena. "I live between the seams with three ways of living battling for my soul." She gazed for a moment at the moon spilling its light across the landscape. "I'm not popular with the other women at Camp Verde. All they see is a Comanche."

"Everybody has to be somebody. It's what you do that counts," said Matthews.

"I want to teach children to read and write. I jumped at the chance to ride along with the surveying wagon to Fort Lancaster then on to El Paso." Her eyes sparkled like dark, shiny pools as she spoke.

He imagined the little town of El Paso as a dusty outpost with adobe homes, scattered ranches, and a mix of Spanish, Mexican, and Anglo-Americans scratching out an existence. Would they have time for education?

Matthews shared his boyhood memories of growing up in a one-room cabin in Tennessee. How the itch to see what's over the next hill led him to Texas and the Army.

LIEUTENANT STANTON ISSUED terse orders in the rose-colored predawn light.

Lieutenant Hancock rested his clasped hands on his rounding stomach and shared his dislike of the heat with Perkins, his civilian surveyor companion. Hancock's round face had a waterfall of a dark mustache salted with gray.

Perkins was thinner and older than Hancock. He nodded his long, sad face as if they were discussing a death in the family. Perkins had a pronounced Adams' apple that bobbed when he swallowed. Bulging veins and brown age spots littered the backs of his hands.

"First Sergeant Matthews! Where are the camels?" Lieutenant Stanton shouted across the parade ground.

"Sir!" said Mathews as a camel handler guided six pack-carrying camels out of the corral. Matthews listened to the handler curse in broken English while he prodded the camels forward.

The handler wore red pants, boots, and a patched wool shirt. He clutched a gray blanket around his shoulders at the throat with one hand.

Matthews mounted a tough sorrel gelding he knew could handle the hard, rocky ride ahead. He glimpsed, in the brightening day, Lena getting into the back of the surveyor wagon. Lieutenant Stanton had a hand on her elbow, assisting.

"Mount and move out." Stanton shouted the order. Perkins slapped the reins on the mules' backsides to start them in motion. Matthews fell in with the other nine troopers around the wagon.

They left hours before reveille and flag raising. The Camp Verde sentries were the only ones up to wish them good luck. The eight-day journey to Fort Lancaster would be another test of camels in the harsh Texas terrain.

They traveled at a mule's pace over rolling hills covered in patchy grass and scrub for over a week. It was a sun-scorched land of rock and sand, mesquite and greasewood. As the terrain became hilly, cedar and live oak dotted the landscape.

Matthews snatched precious moments to talk with Lena during the mild Texas evenings.

One day, Trooper Cotton came back from a scout with pronghorn meat tied to his saddle. Cotton answered the back slaps from the other soldiers with a shy smile on his boyish face.

Late in the afternoon and a day and a half out from Fort Lancaster, Trooper Jennings came thundering back to the caravan, his mount's lips flecked with foam. He stopped short in front of Matthews and saluted, saying, "Comanche!"

Lieutenant Stanton nudged his way between the sergeant and Jennings. "Report, Trooper!"

"Twenty Comanche. Raiding party. Looks like they're fixin' for a fight."

"Form up the men, Sergeant."

"Sir, are you attacking? They have two to one odds." The comment slipped out of his mouth.

"Are you disobeying an order, First Sergeant?" A shrill tightness registered in his voice.

"No, sir. I respectfully suggest we dismount and take cover. We have ammunition and good cover. We have civilians with us and it will be nighttime soon."

Stanton ignored the advice. "Men, form a line on me and prepare to charge!" Whipping his horse around, he shouted at Matthews, "See to the wagon and camels!" The lieutenant's eyes cast a feverish glint as he yanked his pistol out of its holster.

Matthews raced back to the wagon.

"What's that dang fool going to do?" asked Perkins. "He's not going to charge a bushel of Comanche?"

"Pull the wagon back behind the rocks for cover." Matthews gestured to a rocky outcropping extending up a few feet from the ground.

"Lena?" he poked his head inside the wagon's canvas covering for a moment.

"Lieutenant Hancock gave me this." She looked down at a Model 1851 Navy Revolver in her lap. "My father taught me how to shoot."

Matthews helped her out of the wagon and guided her to the ground beneath the wagon. "Keep your head down!"

Matthews snatched a glance at the full, bright moon just visible in the darkening sky. A Comanche Moon.

On his stomach behind rocks, Hancock inserted a paper cartridge into his Sharps rifle and set the percussion cap. Perkins unhitched the mules.

Lieutenant Stanton was twenty yards ahead, waving the troopers forward at a trot. Matthews's heart bounced inside his chest like a nervous cat.

The Comanche appeared like phantoms on horseback. They fired arrows and shook their lances decorated with feathers and carvings before turning and galloping away. Stanton screamed, his voice pitched higher, "After 'em boys! Charge!"

"No!" yelled Matthews. His guts turned cold.

He heard Sharps carbine rounds fired, then all went silent. A handful of heartbeats later, three horsemen galloped back.

Wilcox, Jennings, and Cotton pulled up next to the surveyor wagon. The horses' flanks shuddered with labored breathing.

"It was a trap," said Wilcox, sliding out of the saddle.

"How many?" asked Matthews.

"Too many, Sarge," Jennings said. Sweat plastered his red hair to his head. "I'd rather be cleaning latrines right now."

In the bright light of a Comanche Moon, a lean, bare-chested warrior rode forward. Blood dripped down the arm holding a fresh blond scalp high in the air for all to see.

"Cotton!" yelled Matthews. "Can you hit that Indian riding in the front?"

Matthews crawled over to Cotton.

"I never killed nobody before," Cotton replied.

"Cotton, if you don't kill him, he'll be parading around with your scalp next. Shoot him. You're our best shot."

Cotton swallowed and bench-rested the rifle on a rock. The Comanche were waving new scalps when the boom from Cotton's Sharps rifle sliced the air.

The Comanche with the blonde scalp slumped. He grabbed his horse's mane and rode away, hanging over the horse's neck.

"It gets easier, Trooper," said Matthews. A deep weariness in his muscles and bones passed over him.

Does it get easier or do you become numb to it?

He crawled back to Lieutenant Hancock and looked into his broad, careful face.

"I'm ranking officer now, but I'm a surveyor that happens to be in the Army. I bow to your experience."

"Comanche attack on horseback with bows and lances," said Matthews. "Perkins, watch our back door and guard the mules and horses. Wilcox, help him out."

His eyes sought out Lena. He gazed an instant at her coal black hair, supple brown throat, and lips, red as an apple. He had a pang of regret, and then the arrows were as thick as flies.

Wiry Comanche warriors with painted faces and chests materialized as if conjured. The Comanche rode their horses like they were one, circling and dodging as their screams echoed off the Comanche Moon.

"Pick your targets! Make 'em count!" Matthews fired his Sharps. The butt slammed back into his shoulder.

"Michael?" said Lena. He turned his head. She was staring at Lieutenant Hancock. Two arrows stuck out of his chest. His eyes were wide open, staring at nothing.

Lena swung her pistol toward Matthews and flame shot out of the barrel, followed by a deafening report. Behind Matthews, a Comanche warrior turned his pony away, dropping his lance. Blood ran down his leg.

Matthews scrambled to where the camel handler was crouched, shaking with fear. Matthews pantomimed what he wanted to do. The handler cursed but formed the roaring, spitting camels into a rough line facing the Comanche.

"Jennings, get over here! Perkins, saddle three mules and get the horses. We're leaving the wagon."

Matthews peered down his rifle's open sights and squeezed off a round at the swirling horde of Comanche with feathers and animal bones flashing in their waist length hair. Intricate bead work on their leggings and moccasins glinted in the light of the Comanche Moon.

"Mount up!" said Matthews.

The camels were roaring and squealing, shaking their enormous heads while the handler used a goading stick to prod the camels toward the Comanche, massing for another charge. The handler shouted a command followed by a series of sharp whistles. An arrow in the throat silenced him.

The Comanches saw the camels and hesitated. Then their horses caught a whiff of the unfamiliar smell of the camels coming at them and panicked. Horses slammed into each other and bucked in a swirling mass of confusion. The horses scattered and retreated as the camels raced forward in a frenzy of biting, stomping, and growling.

FIFTEEN HOURS OF looking back over his shoulder, past a hundred places Comanche could wait in ambush, Matthews's group straggled in to Fort Lancaster. Matthews reported to the post commander, and a patrol left to retrieve the wagon.

The next day, Lena met Matthews leaving the post commander's office.

"The captain told me the Comanche burned the wagon. The camels are nowhere to be found," said Matthews.

"Those poor men. I can't stop thinking about them," said Lena. "Are you re-enlisting in the Army you love so well?"

"That's why I met with the captain. I told him no. It's time to try civilian life."

A smile spread over her face.

"Are you still going to El Paso to teach?" asked Matthews.

"Yes."

" I have back pay coming plus another month due me. I'm thinking about buying a plot of land and trying ranching."

"I hear El Paso is a growing town. You could get a good deal for land."

"That's what I was thinking."

———————

—*R. K. Olson is a multiple award-winning short story and novel writer in the western, pulp and sword & sorcery genres. He has published a dozen short stories. His first novel will be published in 2025 by Two Gun Publishing. Titled Siege at the Slash B, it is a traditional western set in the New Mexico Territory of the early 1880s. The story revolves around a massive land swindle that sparks a range war with plenty of bullets, bare knuckles and bushwhacking. This is the first book in the Roddy Rodriguez Saddle Tramp Hero series.*

Olson started writing after a successful global technology career that had him working on every continent but Antarctica. He lives and writes near the Atlantic Ocean in the New England region of the United States. Check out R. K. Olson's Facebook page: Facebook, website: www.rkolson.net and Amazon Author Page

The Emigrants by Frederic Remington

THE UNBLEMISHED DRESS OF MEREDITH MURRAY

BARLOW CRASSMONT

HIS FINGERS WERE damp long before Mrs. Murray's soft hand shook them.

"How do you do, ma'am?" Wilson Buckley asked. His brow was covered with excessive perspiration. It would be easy to blame it on the mid-summer heat.

"I'm fine, especially knowing I'll have Arizona's finest as protection," the woman said, flashing her white smile. Buckley had seldom seen such stainless teeth, and the awareness made him ashamed of his own smile—crooked and stained and brown in all the places where hers was straight and pearly.

Mrs. Murray noticed the bandage on his left hand. The dry blood had turned dark, nearly black. Her apparent apprehension was too noticeable for him to ignore.

"Don't you worry, Missus Murray," he said. "I shoot with the other hand." She smiled again, and, by grazing his arm in appreciation, made concealed hairs on it stand. He couldn't help but stare at her as she stepped away to pack the last of her things before departure.

It was just as well, for Buckley stared at her fancy dress with a newfound fervor. All he'd known of women were those one paid for in mining town brothels and the travelling widowed squaw who'd offer herself to him for an extra blanket or two before the first snowfall. Yet here was a lady, a noblewoman, something folks in big cities bowed to and took their hats off in front of. Wilson Buckley had never been in the presence of one. He'd only seen paintings of them at that hotel in Yucatan when he served under General Herring back in '47. The Spanish artwork above the hotel's reception desk he'd stared at that evening portrayed a woman of Mrs. Murray's class and elegance, sporting a fancy hat and an umbrella of similar make he'd just seen her carry.

When informed a few days ago of his upcoming assignment, Buckley never imagined he'd be infected with instant infatuation that injected his stomach with a fistfull of butterflies.

"Guess what?" Captain Gaines said to Buckley two days prior, as the latter was filling up his canteen at Stormtrail Stone's water pump. "Your unemployment is officially over." Buckley's eyes lit up at the announcement. 'Bout time. Been sitting around long enough, and there haven't been any bounties to chase.

"What's the job?" he asked. "Another cattle drive?"

"Nah, it's way simpler. Lieutenant Colonel Roger Murray is stationed up at Fort Ironwood, a three day ride from here. His wife just arrived in town, all the way from the East. I need you to escort her out there. Four locals will accompany you, including the driver of her coach, with plenty of supplies."

"Murray?" Buckley said. "You mean….?"

Gaines nodded. "Yup. Murdering Murray—the one and only. Just don't mention that in his presence."

"So we'd be riding on the Riverside Route? Is it safe?"

Gaines nodded. "Local natives have been peaceful. The aggressive ones lie thirty miles south, according to our scouting reports. You should be fine, seeing how the five of you will be armed to the teeth as is. Just get her there safely in one piece. Keep her out of the dust as much as possible. You know how Murray hates dirt."

Their subsequent handshake was the equivalent of pen to paper on the figurative contract, but a poor precursor for the euphoric elation

Buckley would feel when shaking the grandiose woman's hand for the first time. Whereas Gaines' hand was a promise of a monetary compensation that would ensure him of a new pair of trousers and a better pair of boots upon the mission's completion, Mrs. Murray's face and soft skin was a revelation of an angelic presence on earth.

She's the most beautiful thing I've ever seen. How could she ever have married that brute?

***

MRS. MURRAY'S JOURNEY to meet her husband began on July nineteenth, as agreed by all parties. Her coach was small, its exterior brown paint peeling in parts, and its four wheels creaked and croaked like a pair of disagreeable crows. But it rode rather smoothly, all things considered, ensuring the woman's long term comfort. That's all that mattered. Stability. Appearances were irrelevant—unless we're talking about people. The driver, Elliot Newman, was grayer and more seasoned than the last General that Buckley had served under. He drank little, spoke even less, and ate not at all. The only thing that entered his mouth was a thumb's size of tobacco, which he chewed excessively, then spat every which way—once even striking the side of the coach, without even realizing it.

Buckley, for his part, was more than insistent on making sure the lady was comfortable. Morning, noon, evening—even after they'd camped for the night, on a small hill—he made sure she had all she needed.

"Water? Coffee? Tea? A bread roll? Some beef jerky? You name it, ma'am, and you'll have it."

"Thank you, Mister Buckley, but I'm afraid I'll be turning in. I wish you a good night." She nodded, then vanished into the tiny tent his men had set-up for her. Meanwhile, the men made due with playing a little harmonica, courtesy of Drew Barnes, singing several verses of long forgotten songs—"Sally Sunrise Steals Sam's Saddle" with acoustics by the youngest of the bunch, Raylee Church. Old man Newman and Charlie Lyons chewed tobacco and passed a bottle of brandy back and forth for the longest, until drunkenness and fatigue nudged them into a deep sleep, after which their snoring and intermittent flatulences were the only signs of their existence.

Buckley kept the first watch. Staring at the stars, he tried picturing Mrs. Murray's face as the grandest of all constellations. Her dress reminded him of the unsullied clouds that gracefully hovered and often generated a much needed shade from the merciless sun, her eyes the purest of blue skies. The bright moon stood for a large jewel that he could effortlessly pick and attach to a golden ring, then place around her delicate finger. The fantastical projection of her jubilant reaction made his heart soar, and the ensuing caress of his face by her gentle hand made him giddy and excited, even giggly. Yeah, that'll be the day. But with her husband's position, one never knew. Army men were always at risk, especially in these lawless lands.

After he unknowingly closed his eyes, Buckley dreamt the sweetest dreams. So what if they were rooted in unrealistic fantasy? He fell asleep on watch and was embarrassed, but no one noticed.

———————•⟨⟨⊗⟩⟩•———————

THE FOLLOWING AFTERNOON the group passed the town of Winslow and saw several natives hovering in the surrounding hills. Perched atop their horses, the Indians moved not a muscle, waved not a limb, nor wiggled a solitary finger. Buckley watched them with his mouth slightly ajar, frustrated by not being able to recognize their tribe.

"Are those the Reckless Snake's warriors?" he asked Barnes. The other merely shrugged.

"From this distance, it's hard to tell." Alarmed at the wagon's slowing pace, Mrs. Murray stuck her head out of the window. Buckley's momentary apprehension soon showed on her own face. Of late, she was quick to mirror her main guardian's demeanor.

"Take Lyons and an extra bottle, and go see what's what. Approach slowly, with your hands up. Be kind and friendly. We don't want any trouble. Tell them we mean no harm. Just passin' through."

Barnes nodded, and soon a dust cloud was all him and Lyons left in their wake as they rode in the direction of the native on the nearest hill. Buckley and Church stood side by side, watching unwaveringly. Newman spat black, loathsome tobacco. Mrs. Murray's face did little to conceal her worry.

"Mister Buckley," she said. "Should we be worried?"

"No, ma'am," he replied. "Everything's under control. Do you need anything? Water?"

She shook her head, then asked, "Are we close to the Fort?"

"We should be halfway there in a few hours, provided we're not delayed too much longer." Buckley turned to Church, who was already on the binoculars, aimed at their friends in the distance.

"Talk to me," Buckley said.

"They're there. Barnes is talkin' to the Injun." The moments of silence between each new development made Buckley swallow excessively. Part of him would've preferred a torture totem to this, especially in the woman's presence. If they were only travelling solo, without the Colonel's wife, the anxiety would be of another nature. Non-existent, perhaps. Tough cowboys and gunslingers hardly feared a few natives here and there, but when women were involved, it was a different story. Yet Gaines told him it was safe, that there wasn't anything to fear. Why would he have lied, if it weren't so?

"They're laughing," Church said. "A jovial trio is a good sign. Lyons gave the Injun the bottle. The man looks so happy he could kiss him." Buckley breathed a sign of relief.

"All right," Church said. "Our boys are giving me the thumbs up sign. All is well, boss."

Thank goodness.

But Buckely was barely able to tell the lady that the situation was under control before the first shots were fired. Their echoes hadn't even settled when Raylee Church screamed, "Holy shit!" The words sent chills though Buckley and Mrs. Murray.

"They shot them," Church yelled. "They shot them both, boss!"

"Who?" Buckley cried. "Who did?"

"That bastard wasn't alone—his warriors were hiding behind the stones. They got more than arrows and spears—I see rifles. Plenty of 'em!" He put the binoculars down and rushed toward the wagon. "Let's move! They're coming this way!"

The final syllable was completed before Church's head was blown off by a nearby shotgun. As his body collapsed, Newman was shot several times from the same direction, his decrepit body taking seconds to gracefully strike the ground, like a sack too lazy to land in a timely manner.

Mrs. Murray screamed. Her shriek echoed across the land, piercing through Buckley's heart worse than a poisoned arrow. Everything was spinning out of control—his world, his mind, his life. The continued wailing of the lady did little to alleviate the internal mayhem.

"Drop your gun, or die," a voice said from behind him. "Turn around—but do it slowly."

Buckley did as told. For his effort, he was rewarded with the sight of five men. Two were natives of unknown origin, two were white guns for hire—apparent in the numerous pistols on their belts and skeptical countenances. One was a Mestizo, an offspring of a Mexican and an American Indian. His skin was almond colored, and his hair darker than night.

One of the purer Natives approached on his unsaddled horse. He was as confident as the wind and just as unpredictable—an older man possessing long shiny hair, with a face that might as well have been carved from stone. Scarred and mutilated in several places, the man's stare possessed an iron grip that made Buckley's stomach turn.

"Identify yourself," the Mestizo said.

"Wilson Buckley. Who are you?"

"We're asking the questions. Where are you headed?"

"I can't tell you that."

"Even if I threaten to shoot the woman?"

Buckley lifted his arms further up, waving them agreeably.

"We were told these lands were safe," Buckley said.

"If you were told a fairy tale before bedtime, would you believe it to be real?"

Two of the group stormed the stagecoach and dragged Mrs. Murray out. She was screaming, yelling, and pleading for help. If only I could. But what would be the point? They'd shoot us both.

This way, we might have a chance. Maybe.

One of the men placed her on a horse, holding a knife next to her throat. He not only ignored her wailing—he seemed to take pleasure in it. The others disarmed Buckley, taking every firearm he had.

"You're coming with us," the Mestizo said. "Both of you. You try anything, you die. Understand?" Buckley nodded. He glanced at the woman whose face was consumed with tears. But his shame was so great that he could not but look away, crippled by a growing remorse. Hoods were placed on Buckley and Mrs. Murray's heads, and soon the new party was on their way. The gunslinger rode in the middle of the murdering cavalry, multiple gun barrels pointed at him—and the terrified woman he was assigned to protect.

THE AIR COOLED and became thinner as the group rode on for several hours.

There was a noticeable ascension up a hill or a mountain or what have you—Buckley could not tell. Still, the elements were changing drastically. At length, the woman's sobs became subdued, and soon she was merely sniffling in lieu of weeping loudly in desperation. Goddamn that Gaines. Why the hell would he send us out into hostile lands? And where could they be taking us?

In over an hour's time, Buckley's eyes were no wiser as to where they had arrived when they finally stopped. The aroma of burning wood infiltrated his nostrils, and a faint taste of broiled meat hung heavy in the air. His feet made crunchy noises on the unknown terrain after he dismounted his horse. He heard Mrs. Murray's moans once again, and her cries faded as she was led away from him. Entering a large enclosure, he noticed the breeze vanish and no longer heard the wailing wind. Warmth overwhelmed him, and his captors made him sit down, without taking the hood off his head.

When he suddenly inquired, "Where have you brought us?", all he got in return was a kick to his ribcage, and a brutish shut up, before he quickly complied. The captor in question shut the door, leaving Buckley alone in the small room, his hands and feet bound in a most uncomfortable manner. He was instantly tormented with the unbearable weight of remorse and regretful thoughts. How could I have been so stupid? We were a day away from the fort, and four men are now dead. They'll likely kill us as well. Not sure why they haven't done it already.

Hours dragged on laboriously, with the sluggishness of long nights during wintertime. Buckley heard—through a wall or canopy or whatever barrier separated them Mrs. Murray's cries intermittently—she pleaded and begged and asked for mercy. But all her requests were quickly extinguished. Each cry she emitted cut through Buckley's heart like a knife inserted handle deep, then twisted continuously. He closed his eyes, hoping his tightly shut eyelids would conceal the horrible sounds that his poor judgment had led them to. If that was their objective, why did they bring him along? Why didn't they shoot him, as they had done the other four?

Night was deep in the making when another pair of boots announced their arrival in his small enclosure. There was a clinking of a plate or a cup or a pot placed on the wooden floor. Its enticing aroma made Buckley's starving stomach envious.

"I've brought you food and drink," a voice said. "I've two pistols, locked and loaded. Understand?" Buckley was seasoned enough to know that toughness and bravery were admirable qualities, but this was not a time to succumb to either. Life, despite its current setback, was preferable to death, regardless of his current anger and resentment. So he nodded, as feebly as a starving sheep.

His hood was taken off, and his eyes gradually adjusting to the light he'd not seen for nearly a day, revealed the face of the familiar Mestizo.

"Eat," the man said. Buckley reached for the bowl, where a crusty piece of bread lay over a brown steaming stew. Asking what was in there would've been fruitless, so he proceeded to shamelessly stuff his mouth. He ate heartily, like an uncultured brute. But he didn't care, especially after all he'd been through. I'll need strength if I stand a chance of getting out of here should an opportunity present itself. The other's eyes were on him, cool and cautious.

"Why did you bring us here?" Buckley asked, when his plate was almost empty.

"Chief Yellow Worm is carrying out his revenge," Mestizo said.

Buckley tried to picture the face of the old native he saw before they were taken away. It struck him as a haunting painting of muted wrath. "Revenge? On who?"

"On the murdering colonel who's wiped out his entire tribe."

"Colonel Murray?"

"The natives have a different name for that monster—as do some of your people."

"What's he going to do?"

"To you—nothing. But to the man's wife—well, that's up to him."

"Please." Buckley pleaded, raising his hands. "Please, do not hurt her. Please!"

"I have no say. Yellow Worm is in charge, and his wounds run deep."

"Please!" Buckley cried, raising his voice. "Take me! Take me instead, just let her go! I beg of you!"

The Mestizo chuckled, shaking his head. "I doubt you're the chief's type. Neither is she, to be honest, but she's the only connection to the monster who's destroyed all the chief holds dear."

Buckley watched the man's countenance with an uncomfortable knot in his stomach. All the food he'd just wolfed down felt as if it would shoot back up and blow itself on the man's rugged boots. He tried to shake the horror away and focus on other matters, but under the circumstances, the nausea refused to budge.

"Taking advantage of a defenseless woman," Buckley said. "Some tough guy your chief is. If he wants revenge, why not attack the Fort and take it out on the one responsible?"

"He will—in time. Our numbers and weapons are currently no match for the white man's army, but once we form alliances with the northwest tribes, we may stand a chance."

"So why not wait and do that, without tormenting a woman who had nothing to do with it? She doesn't deserve any punishment."

"Neither did Yellow Worm's people. His wife and daughters were burned alive by the Colonel, along with a hundred others. Not only has he not been punished for those crimes, he roams about freely, collecting badges for every native he cuts down."

"Many of us don't agree with what he's done," Buckley said. "Why resort to similar atrocities?"

"We're not—not exactly," the Mestizo said. "The Colonel's wife will not suffer as the Chief's family. But a point has to be made, a justice of some sort. We don't expect you to understand."

The man placed the hood back on Buckley's head and left. Buckley spent the night dreaming the stuff of nightmares, the quiet howling of a woman's suffering never giving him a moment's peace.

THE FOLLOWING MORNING he woke with bloodshot eyes and was dragged outdoors. Mounted on his horse again, his captors led him away for several hours, before the hood was finally removed. The Mestizo stood next to him, along with another native. On another horse, Mrs. Murray sat, motionless as a mountain. Her eyes were red, her face covered in bruises. She wore a dark, rugged blanket, which wrapped her from neck to foot.

"Missus Murray," Buckley said. "Are you...?" There was no point in completing the query. The woman was beaten, body and soul, barely any light left in her dim eyes.

"Your fort will be a six hour ride, that way," the Mestizo said, pointing in that direction. "You have two canteens and a clear path. We'll make sure you reach the destination unharmed." He handed Buckley an additional sack, then said, "Her dress."

Unharmed? Too late for that.

The Mestizo and his companion left. Buckley guided his horse toward Mrs. Murray. He looked at her, but she didn't glance back. Her eyes looked at nowhere and no one—at nothing whatsoever. Buckley took her horse's reins and gently yanked it, propelling it to move in the right direction. They were on their way—somber as a two-person funeral procession.

———————◆◆◆———————

THEY REACHED FORT Ironwood in the predicted time. The soldiers on sentry were surprised to see only two riders, when they'd expected five, in addition to the carriage. Buckley struggled to explain himself while yelling upwards to the men at the gate. His voice was broken, shaky, and demolished.

"I'm Wilson Buckley, escorting Missus Murray. We were ambushed. Several casualties. Let us inside, please."

As the large gate finally opened, Colonel Murray ran toward his wife, agitated and disheveled. He sucked air in large gulps like someone who'd just completed a marathon.

"What happened?" he cried, his stare going from his wife to Wilson Buckley. "What happened to her? Where are the others?" Colonel Murray attempted speaking to his wife, but even after several questions, got no response from her. Buckley tried intervening with details, but the Colonel just waved him off, uninterested.

At length, the husband helped his wife off the horse, and, whispering soothing words into her ear, led her to his quarters. She was breathing, and her eyes were open, but otherwise walked as the living dead. Gliding, while her limbs stagnated as deceased branches. Buckley watched her vanish in the distance, fighting long suppressed tears.

A young soldier, sporting several pimples on his pale youthful face, walked up to Buckley.

"What the hell happened?" he asked. "She looks like she went through hell."

Putting it mildly.

Buckley handed him the sack, then said, "Her dress. See that the Colonel gets it."

The soldier glanced at it, then asked, "Why isn't she wearing it?"

Buckley walked away, fruitlessly trying to conceal the shame that hung like an albatross around his neck. The soldier, meanwhile, opened the sack, and unfolded the dress. It stood as spotless as ever, without the tiniest blemish, nearly glowing under the late afternoon sun.

When Buckley glanced at it for the final time, he only wished that his conscience possessed such an unsullied, flawless quality.

———————⊰⊱———————

—*Barlow Crassmont has lived in the USA, Eastern Europe, Middle East, and China. When not teaching or writing, he dabbles in juggling, solving the Rubik's Cube, and learning other languages.*

Son of immigrant parents, a Bosnian mother and a Palestinian father, he moved from Europe to America when he was thirteen and has never looked back. He fell in love with cinema, literature, and tennis at an early age, and although he'd have liked to make a living in the other two industries, writing became the only realistic, affordable escape to live out one aspect of his adolescent passions.

He has been published by British Science Fiction Association, Mobius Blvd, Forest Publications, Mania Magazine, The Literary Times, Nine Muses Review, Rethink Magazine, Haunted Portal Magazine, Ghost City Review, Hot Pot Magazine, Amsterdam Quarterly, Daikaijuzine, The Creekside Magazine, Blue Moon Review, MoonLit Getaway, Culterate Magazine, *and in the 41st anthology of* Writers of the Future.

THE PRIEST WITH NO NAME

ALBERT MORROW

THE CIRCUMSTANCES BEHIND "Whiskey Red" Fallow wearing the stolen habit of a Catholic priest could fill a book. His life was full of bad choices that often led to lies and crimes and rapid flights from posses whose zeal for capturing him was unnerving. It would take fewer words to detail the life of the poor holy man whose unfortunate encounter with Red ended with him fleeing across a field in his underdrawers. That unfortunate cleric isn't the central character of this story, though.

This story is about Red and his problem getting his Remington .44 situated under his purloined priestly apparel. The revolver would only stay truly out of sight if he shoved his belt around sideways and wore it over his middle. That was uncomfortable, and he couldn't get to it with any speed, but no one was ever going to look for Red dressed as a priest.

"So long as I can make it to the Mexican border, I don't care if I have to leave my gun behind and go in my underdrawers," he said to himself. "I just wish I knew which direction to take to get there."

The opposite direction of the posse seemed a natural choice, and he set his mind to dreaming up a story to explain why a priest was walking alone under the Arizona Territory sun. The heat beat a good idea into his head, and he decided to tell the truth, part of it, anyway.

"It seems I had an encounter with that dashing and daring outlaw, 'Whiskey Red' Fallow," he decided. "He robbed me of my horse and lit out for Tennessee."

He practiced telling the story as he walked. He entered a forest after a few miles and was glad to be under the shelter of foliage.

"This priest's getup is awful stuffy," he said to a squirrel eating an acorn on a low branch. "It ain't no wonder them religious fellows is always in such bad moods if they got to put up with these clothes."

He couldn't get his Remington out to shoot the squirrel, so he flipped sweat from his forehead at it. The moisture fell well short, and the squirrel scampered up the tree unharmed.

Movement coming through the forest drew Red's notice then, and his hand went to his side. When he touched only black cloth, he cussed and went under his habit for his Remington. That turned out to be more difficult than expected with the result being that he was twisted up like a pretzel with his hand clawing around under his clothes when a small boy stepped in front of him.

Red yanked his hand free and untwisted his body as the boy blinked his eyes in confusion.

"Father?" he said. "My daddy needs you."

The boy grabbed Red's hand and pulled with all the strength of his thin, frail body. Red could easily have resisted him, but he didn't. He let the child drag him into the forest.

"Daddy's hurt," the boy said. "Some bad men shot him."

Red pulled up, jerking the boy to a halt. "Shot? Who shot him?"

"Some bad men who think Daddy has money hid. Come on, please. Daddy needs you."

"I don't know what I can do for him," Red mumbled and then said louder, "Money? Does your dad have some money hid?"

"The bad men think he does. Only Daddy knows."

"Let's get to him then," said Red, letting the boy drag him onward. The trees opened up suddenly, and they entered a clearing. A dilapidated cabin of log and mud with a thatched roof sat in the middle of it.

That's an unlikely place to find any amount of money worth shooting a man over.

He followed the boy through the scrap of animal hide that served as a door. The inside smelled damp and moldy and was dimly lit by a lantern dangling from a water-damaged rafter.

A man with a stinking gut wound lay on a bed of straw. A woman with stringy hair hovered by his side. Her body was bony, and her face thin and pale. She looked up as they entered.

"I got someone to help Daddy, Momma," the boy said.

The woman blew out a scoffing breath. "A priest will do him more good than a doctor now, but your daddy ain't likely to confess nothin'," she said.

The boy turned his face to Red, nevertheless. The bright expectation writ there was too much for Red to bear, and he shied away. He went to the bedside. The man's shirt and the straw around his middle were wet with dark blood, and the blood stink was heavier up close.

She's right. This man is dead. He just don't know it yet.

The woman shook the man's shoulder and said, "Teddy."

The man's eyes opened. They were lit with something that was either delirium or relief. Red couldn't tell which.

"I only ever done one really bad thing, Father," Teddy said. The woman interrupted him with a scoffing laugh.

Red waved her silent. He didn't know that a priest could get him to confess anything that a man with a gun hadn't, but he was sure going to try. He knelt over the man and made some motions he had seen a Lutheran preacher do and said, "Latta matta hootcha moocha."

Hoping that sounded churchy enough, he clasped his hands together and said, "You need to get whatever is troubling you off your chest, cuz you ain't got much time left, my son."

"I've done bad, Father."

"I heard that part," Red cut in. "What have you done to get you shot?"

"He stole heist money right out of his partners' hands," said a man entering through the hide door. He had a long-barreled Colt revolver pointed at the dying man. To Red, who was so close to the dying man they were almost touching, the black end of that barrel looked as big as a train tunnel.

I'm standing on those tracks about to be hit.

Two more men came in. Red couldn't pull his gaze away from the Colt enough to tell for certain, but he figured they had drawn guns as well.

"Don't hurt my daddy!" the boy suddenly yelled.

He moved toward the men, who reacted with the reflexes of lawless men and moved their gun sights to him. Red used that moment to stand. His only goal was to get away from the dying man. He bumped into the boy, however, and knocked him to the floor.

"Sorry, kid," he said.

He helped the boy to his feet and was startled to see that three gun barrels were now aimed at him.

"Hey now, there ain't no need for that," he said. "I mean, violence don't need to be... done here in this place. You are in no danger... my sons."

The dying man's hidden stash was no longer of any particular importance to Red. Getting out of the cabin alive was his goal now. Absent-mindedly, he pushed the child toward his mother, trying to come up with words that would prevent any gunfire.

"You can put those guns—those implements of devilry—away," he said. "You don't need them here. These poor... servants of God have nothing to tempt you to acts of, uh... crime and villainy."

"Shut your mouth, God man," said the first man in the door.

The second man, a blond fellow with a shaggy beard, cut in with, "Watch your words, Aaron. You shouldn't talk that way to a priest."

"Yeah," agreed the third man, a burly guy in a denim vest. "That's a sin or something, I think."

"I've done worse," said Aaron, the leader.

"But we ain't," said Shaggy Beard. Denim Vest nodded in agreement and lowered his revolver. Shaggy Beard did likewise.

Aaron did not. He waved his revolver about the room, shouting, "I'm going to get my money! Someone's going to give it up if I have to shoot everyone here to get it."

"Th-that would only m-make your c-crimes worse, my son," Red stuttered out. "Do not add to your time in the fires of the inferno."

Aaron gave Red a dirty look and aimed the gun at him.

Red cursed himself for a fool who never knew when to shut up and tried not to look at the gun barrel.

"How can he add to his time in the lake of fire?" asked Shaggy Beard.

"Yeah," said Denim Vest. "I thought it was an all-or-nothing kind of thing. If you went... there... you just burned without ever burning away?"

How am I supposed to know? I ain't been to church enough to know these things.

"The fires," he suddenly said as inspiration hit him, "do burn forever, but the fires can be hotter for those whose sins are... worse than others."

"Yeah," said Shaggy Beard. "Yeah, that makes sense."

"Like a campfire for stealing and bonfire for killing," replied Denim Vest.

"Yes, my sons," said Red, mentally breathing a sigh of relief.

"What do you think lying gets you?" asked Shaggy Beard.

"I don't know," replied Denim Vest. "Maybe something like a brush fire. You know, they burn quick but ain't real hot."

"That sounds about right," said Shaggy Beard. "Is that right, Father?"

"Shut up!" yelled Aaron. "All of you! We ain't in church!"

Before he could stop himself, something that Red had heard often as a child flew out of his mouth. "God is everywhere, my son. He walks among us at all times. He sees everything we do."

"He's about to see me shoot a mouthy priest," Aaron growled.

Red couldn't have talked then. Aaron's finger was on the trigger, and Red knew how little pressure it took to cause a trigger to break.

If he even breathes too hard, I'm dead.

"What if you killed someone but you didn't mean to?" asked Denim Vest.

"What are you going on about?" Aaron's eyes went to Denim Vest, but his revolver stayed pointed at Red. "If I kill someone, I mean to do it. I've done it before, and I'll do it again if I have to."

"No, what he means is, what if some person kills a man he didn't mean to kill," said Shaggy Beard. "Ain't that right, Dennis?"

"Yep, that's what I meant," replied Denim Vest Dennis. "Like if you was to shoot at someone trying to shoot you and instead hit some guy who wasn't doing nothing but just walking along the street. How hot a fire would that get you?"

Red wasn't about to answer and possibly get shot, but thankfully, Shaggy Beard said, "Something like a house fire around you, maybe. They're hot when you're inside them, but not as hot as the fire that's burning the wood."

"I was in a burning bank once," said Dennis. "I accidentally shot a lantern during a robbery and near burned to death. It was pretty darn hot, but not as bad as a bonfire."

Shaggy Beard nodded. "I was in a barn fire one time. That was probably similar."

"How about I shoot both of you and this priest," said Aaron. "That way I get all the money and ain't got to listen to any more church talk!"

"Sorry, Aaron," said Shaggy Beard. "I just been kind of bothered by stuff like this for a while is all."

"Yeah, me too," said Dennis.

"The money we're owed from this cash-stealing snake will clear all that churchy nonsense out of your heads," Aaron told them. "And I know how to get Teddy to talk."

He turned to the dying man. "He ain't afraid of us. I done killed him with that bullet to his guts. I'll bet he would talk if I start shooting up his brat before he dies though."

His gun barrel moved from Red toward the boy. Red spoke then, crying out without thinking, "You can't do that! Not to a kid!"

Aaron's Colt whipped back to Red, and no other words were said after that. The motion of swinging his Colt around caused Aaron's trigger finger to move just enough. The gun spat fire and lead, and Red went down, clutching his middle.

The lantern broke at nearly the same time, splashing hot burning oil in Aaron's face.

Red gasped on the floor, struggling to get air into his lungs. He felt like he'd been kicked by a mule.

I'm dead! There ain't no way to live from this. I'll die slow and hurt the whole time. It'll be like burning!

It wasn't his belly his hands were holding, though, but something hard.

My Remington! He shot my gun! I'm going to be sore as... that place I ain't about to mention, but I'll live.

Above him, Aaron was screaming about being blind.

"Struck blind!" yelled Shaggy Beard.

"We told him not to shoot that priest!" Dennis said, shouting.

The bullet that hit my Remington must have bounced and hit the lantern. He sat up and got to his feet. The cabin went dead quiet then, and Red looked around to see that all eyes, except for Aaron's, were focused on him.

The woman dropped to her knees, dragging the boy down with her. She began reciting The Lord's Prayer. Seconds later, the boy lowered his head and joined her in prayer. Teddy gasped out his last breath and died gazing skyward with a look of rapture on his face.

Dennis and Shaggy Beard threw their revolvers at Red's feet and fled the cabin, confessing sins and begging for forgiveness in loud, tearful voices. Aaron's vision cleared enough to show him that Red was alive and unharmed before him. His vision went black then, and he fainted to the floor.

Red, not caring one whit for the reactions he caused by not dying, fled the cabin at a full run. He was half a mile away when he began to wrestle free of the priestly garb. He threw the black habit at a tree and chucked his broken Remington at the sun.

He was across the Mexican border three days later, nearly the same time as the bullet-holed habit was found hanging from a tree limb. It was taken to the Church of the Angelic Vision where it is still displayed to this day. Countless visitors have seen it and heard the tale of an unnamed priest who was resurrected, blinded a heretic, and ascended into the sanctity of Heaven, leaving the holey, holy garment behind.

—*Albert Morrow is a freelance writer of feature stories and articles for newspapers of Rust Media and magazines of Best Version Media. In 2023, he received an Honorable Mention in the L. Ron Hubbard Writers of the Future Contest for his novella "Widow's Lament." His stories, "The Cursed Cabin of Cat's Holler" and "Miswritings in the Dark," have won awards in the White County Creative Writers Conferences held in Searcy, Arkansas. The debut book of his paranormal western hero, Dix Dereuse, was released in 2025.*

BIG SKIES. BOLD FLAVORS.
REAL RANCH COOKING.

Will Rogers Medallion Award-winning author **Sherry Monahan** takes you on a delicious ride through the kitchens of America's most iconic dude and guest ranches in the first volume of her new Culinary Treasures cookbook series. From sun-up sourdough flapjacks to sundown skillet suppers, *Dude & Guest Ranches of America* delivers recipes straight from the trail, the chuckwagon, and the family table—each served with a side of Western heritage and hospitality. Learn the secrets of perfect cowboy steaks, campfire beans, and flaky ranch pies, all while exploring the untold stories of the families who keep these living legends alive. Fire up your range and rediscover the spirit of the West—one unforgettable bite at a time.

www.sherrymonahan.com

HAT CREEK

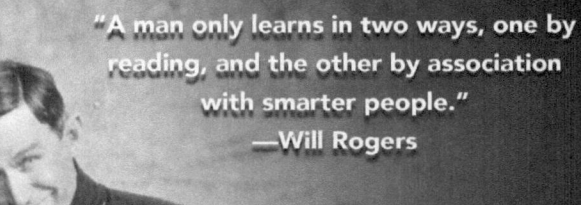

"A man only learns in two ways, one by reading, and the other by association with smarter people."
—Will Rogers

WILL ROGERS
MEDALLION

RECOGNIZING EXCELLENCE IN WESTERN MEDIA AND STORYTELLING AND COWBOY POETRY

www.willrogersmedallionaward.net

THE HAUNTING NEW WESTERN MYSTERY

SHARON
FRAME GAY

WHERE THE
CROWS
FLY

WHERE CROWS GATHER...
DEATH AIN'T FAR BEHIND.

NOW AVAILABE EVERWHERE BOOKS ARE SOLD

MOST MEN WOULD WAIT ON THE LAW.

NOT THIS ONE.